"YOU ALL DON'T LIKE VERONICA MUCH, DO YOU?" MOLLY SAID TO THE YOUNG PRODUCTION ASSISTANT.

"She's making Greg crazy. That's not good for him, and it's not good for the film."

"Why do you suppose she gets to him? Surely, he's worked with other difficult actresses."

"Beats me. I'd have told her to take a hike the first day, but Greg wouldn't budge. He wanted her on this picture no matter what. Fought the studio and everyone else till he got his way." Jerry rapped on the trailer door and waited. When no one answered, he peered inside. "Oh, hell," he muttered, the color draining out of his face. He leaned against the side of the trailer and drew in a couple of deep breaths before shouting at the top of his lungs. "Hank, guys, get the hell over here."

"What is it?" Molly said, trying to peer past him. Jerry blocked her way. He wasn't quite big enough, though, to keep her from spotting one dungaree-clad leg at an awkward angle. She recognized Gregory Kinsey's well-worn cowboy boot. She swallowed hard and forced her eyes away. "Shouldn't you get inside and do something?"

"Sweetheart, there's not much you can do for a guy who's got a bullet wound in the middle of his head."

Dell Books also by Sherryl Woods

HOT PROPERTY

A MOLLY DEWITT ROMANTIC MYSTERY

HOT SECRET

SHERRYL WOODS

A DELL BOOK

Published by
Dell Publishing
a division of
Bantam Doubleday Dell Publishing Group, Inc.
666 Fifth Avenue
New York, New York 10103

The trademark Dell® is registered in the
U.S. Patent and Trademark Office.

ISBN: 0-440-21004-6

Printed in the United States of America

Published simultaneously in Canada

November 1992

10 9 8 7 6 5 4 3 2 1

RAD

HOT
SECRET

CHAPTER
ONE

Anyone who considered filmmaking glamorous had never been on a movie set at the end of a twelve-hour day. And at ten P.M. on a hot and humid Saturday night, tempers tended to be frayed beyond repair. Veronica Weston's dressing room trailer, half a block long and complete with kitchen, practically reverberated with the echoes of an argument that had begun in mid-morning and gotten noisier and nastier with each passing hour. Anyone who knew the gist of the star's complaint wasn't sharing it with Molly DeWitt, who'd been assigned by the Miami/Dade film office to keep everyone happy. Judging from the shouts, she wasn't doing a wonderful job.

Hot, tired, and drained from the nonstop tension, Molly sat at the Cardoza's porchfront café in Miami Beach's rejuvenated Art Deco district and sipped on her tenth iced tea since dinnertime. If she hadn't been working, she would have ordered something a lot more lethal. The thought of a piña colada or maybe a straight shot of Scotch held an almost irresistible appeal.

The door of Veronica's trailer crashed open and the star emerged in a dramatic swirl of hot pink chiffon that was more suited to a boudoir than to a public place. It was not a costume. Veronica dressed to suit her glamorous image.

The actress caught sight of Molly and made a beeline for her table. She flounced into a chair amid a cloud of pink. It was indicative of the neighborhood, a haven for trendy yuppies and high-fashion European models, that no one paid the slightest attention.

"That man," she said in apparent reference to the film's director, Gregory Kinsey, "has the talent of a toad. I will not listen to another word he says."

Since Veronica was making her comeback film after years of alcoholic decline, Molly thought it prudent to suggest a spirit of cooperation. "I'm sure he has your best interests at heart," she said.

"Ha!" Veronica gestured to a passing waiter and ordered a double vodka on the rocks. Apparently she wasn't worried about either slipping off the wagon or falling down drunk in her final shot of the night.

"After all, it's his reputation on the line as well," Molly ventured, feeling infinitely braver since her first observation hadn't drawn fire. She didn't dare suggest that Gregory Kinsey, whose last two pictures had been money-making Academy Award nominees, hadn't needed to take a risk on a woman who'd dragged her own last two films into overbudget box-office debacles.

Besides, she felt a certain amount of sympathy for the fifty-something actress, whose once-gorgeous face and career had been ravaged by alcohol. She admired the spunk it had taken to ignore all of the vicious tabloid gossip and return to the screen in a less than flattering role, a role Kinsey reportedly had fought to offer her. The fact that the two had been at loggerheads since the first day of production was no secret, and Molly wondered why the up-and-coming Gregory had bothered trying to salvage the woman's downsliding career.

Veronica gulped down the drink and ordered another. "You know, dear, you're really wasting your time in this town," she said, giving Molly a critical once-over. "You ought to move to L.A. That's where the industry is. Half the producers in that town would kill to have someone who could keep things organized the way you do. Does that boss of yours, Vince what's-his-name, appreciate you?"

The concept of self-absorbed Vincent Gates displaying gratitude was enough to make Molly smile. "No, but I happen to love Miami," she said. "And I'm not the issue, you are. What will it take to make you happy? Is there something I can do to make this shoot easier on you?"

Veronica seemed startled that anyone honestly cared what she wanted now that her stardom had crashed like a meteor plummeting to earth.

"Maybe you could go talk to Gregory," she said, slowly warming to the idea. "He'd listen to you. He's surrounded by all those sycophants. I haven't seen so much bowing and scraping since I met the queen. Did I ever tell you that story, dear? Well, never mind, now's not the time. You go speak to Gregory and then we'll talk about all that ancient history."

Molly was flattered by Veronica's faith in her persuasiveness, but she seriously doubted that the director was the least bit interested in her amateur opinions. From what she'd observed this past week on the set, Gregory Kinsey had a pretty good idea of exactly what he wanted in every shot. Barely into his thirties and riding an artistic high, he wasn't the type of director to encourage input. "What exactly is the problem between you two?" Molly asked.

"This godawful script is the problem. Have you read it? Does it make a bit of sense to you? No," she answered before Molly could comment. "Of course not. No woman my age is going to chase around after some worthless twerp like Rod Lukens. What kind of name is that anyway? It sounds like some cowboy drifter."

Since the entire plot of *Endless Tomorrows* was created around just such a chase and just such a drifter, Molly couldn't help inquiring, "Why did you take the role, if you hated it so much?"

Veronica directed one of her famous disbelieving glances at Molly. The subtle lift of one delicate brow spoke volumes on-screen and off. "Offers have not exactly been rolling in the last few years. Everybody wants young. Everybody wants sexy. They seem to forget there's an audience out there that's my age, that women my age can be sexy. I figured I owed it to my gender to prove that."

"And you needed the work," Molly dared to guess.

Veronica laughed, a bawdy, raucous sound that carried on the ocean breeze. "Hell, yes, I needed the work. Do you have any idea how much a stay at that de-tox clinic costs?"

"Then I'm surprised you're so anxious to repeat it," Molly said with a pointed look at the second double vodka sitting in front of the actress.

Veronica didn't seem to take offense. "Don't worry about me, honey. I'm just getting my second wind. When Gregory calls for action, I'll be in front of the camera, hitting my mark and delivering my lines, no matter how absurd they are. The bottom line is I'm a professional and Gregory knows it. He's counting on it, in fact. He'll let me rant and rave all I want as long as I show up."

"So the tantrum's just for show?"

"Essentially," she admitted with a shrug. "Maybe he'll make a few little changes to pacify me, but he knows I can't afford to walk away from this project, no matter what I say."

"Then why bother? Doesn't all this arguing upset you? How can you possibly be creative in the midst of all this tension? I can't finish a grocery list if I'm under a lot of stress."

Veronica threw back her head, setting a shoulder-length wave of chestnut hair into sensuous motion. "Tension, honey? You call this tension? This is just a warm-up. You wait until we get to the love scene, and I refuse to get into bed with that sleazy character until he washes that gunk out of his hair."

Molly had to admit that Duke Lane's insistence

on wearing a slicked-back hairstyle for the role of Miami Beach gigolo Rod Lukens was enough to make her own stomach churn. It might, however, be difficult to get him to step out of character in mid-production and wash his hair. "How do you plan on winning that one?" she asked.

"I've been thinking about insisting on a sexy shower scene which includes a bottle of shampoo. What do you think?" There was an impish gleam in Veronica's vivid green eyes as she contemplated the prospect.

Molly grinned back at her. "A stroke of genius."

"Yeah. Now if I could just figure out how to get him to try the mouthwash, too," she said wearily. She finished her drink and glanced at her watch. "What the hell is slowing things down now? God, I hate night shoots. They drag on forever. If the cameras don't roll soon, I'm going to have bags under my eyes the size of airline carryons. Honey, could you go check for me? If we're not starting soon, I'm going back inside to rest."

"No problem," Molly said. "I'll be right back. Any idea where Gregory is?"

"Probably in the production trailer trying to figure out how he got himself mixed up in this dud."

Molly cut through the Saturday night crowd milling along Ocean Drive past the string of hotels that had been painted the colors of dawn on the Atlantic—palest pink, mauve, turquoise, and sun-bleached white. Front porches that had once seen no more action than the squeaking of a rocking chair now served as swank outdoor cafés. Swimming pools had become the focal point of trendy sidewalk bars. On Thirteenth Street, which had been blocked off to accommodate the production, she passed Veronica's trailer and went on to the slightly smaller RV parked in front. A plastic sign declaring GK PRODUCTIONS, ENDLESS TOMORROWS was plastered on the side.

Molly tapped on the trailer door and opened it. A handful of exhausted-looking, jeans-clad men and women were collapsed into the chairs around a rectangular table along one side of the long, narrow room. Several were playing poker, while the others sipped sodas and watched in apparent boredom.

"Anybody in here seen Gregory?" she asked, stepping inside long enough to savor the Arctic temperature.

"He's with Veronica."

"No," Molly said. "She's been outside at one of the cafés with me for the past twenty minutes."

The legs of one tilted-back chair hit the floor with a thud. "Shit, man, not again," assistant director Hank Murdock muttered as he lumbered to his feet. "Come on, guys. Let's go find him."

"Find him?" Molly repeated. "You think he's taken off or something?"

"The street is crawling with broads and bars and bedrooms. Greg's not known for overlooking any of those opportunities, especially when they come in combination," Hank said in weary resignation.

"Does that mean you're going to have to shut down production for the night? Should I tell Veronica she can go back to her hotel?"

"Not yet. Tell her to hang loose. We may get this last shot in yet. Jerry, you check Veronica's trailer just to be sure he's not still in there. That's the last place any of us saw him. Maybe he stuck around to recuperate once Veronica got her claws out of him."

"Don't panic, man," Jerry Shaw said soothingly. "It could be he's with Daniel setting up the next shot."

"I'll check, but I'm not holding my breath."

Molly walked with Jerry as far as the star's trailer. "You all don't like Veronica much, do you?" she said to the young production assistant. He was only twenty-three and a recent UCLA film school grad, but this was his third film with Gregory Kinsey.

"She's making Greg crazy. That's not good for him and it's not good for the film. Other than that, I don't much think about her one way or the other." For his age he managed an incredible air of bored cynicism.

"Why do you suppose she gets to him? Surely, he's worked with other difficult actresses."

"Beats me. I'd have told her to take a hike the first day, but Greg wouldn't budge. He wanted her on this picture no matter what. Fought the studio and everyone else till he got his way." Jerry rapped on the trailer door and waited. When no one answered, he peered inside.

"Oh, hell," he muttered, the color draining out of his face. He leaned against the side of the trailer and drew in a couple of deep breaths before shouting at the top of his lungs. "Hank, guys, get the hell over here."

"What is it?" Molly said, trying to peer past him. Jerry blocked her way. He wasn't quite big enough, though, to keep her from spotting one dungaree-

clad leg at an awkward angle. She recognized Gregory Kinsey's well-worn cowboy boot. She swallowed
hard and forced her eyes away. "Shouldn't you get
inside and do something?"

"Sweetheart, there's not much you can do for a
guy who's got a bullet wound in the middle of his
head."

CHAPTER
TWO

Chaos erupted as word of the shooting spread along Ocean Drive like news of free drinks. Crew members abandoned cameras, lights, and card games to join the shocked, tearful vigil outside Veronica's trailer. Despite Jerry's conviction that Gregory Kinsey was dead, Hank Murdock shoved the young production assistant aside and went into the trailer to check for himself. When he emerged, his own complexion was ashen.

"Greg's dead. He's been shot," he announced, his voice sandpaper rough and unsteady. He shoved his wide, workman's hands into the pockets of his well-worn jeans, but not before Molly saw how they trembled. She was every bit as shaken by Hank's obvious dismay as she had been by the sight of Greg's body sprawled on the floor.

From the first day on the set Hank Murdock had impressed her as the kind of solid, reliable man anyone would want around in an emergency, the kind of man who would be unfazed by any calamity. His calm, easygoing personality was the opposite of Greg's more volatile, creative frenzy. They'd made good partners. Now one of them was dead and the other obviously distraught.

Molly wondered if there was a prayer that the gunshot wound was self-inflicted. There was one school of thought around the set that Veronica could drive the most stable among them to consider ending it all. Molly thought, though, that the director would have aimed the gun at the actress.

"Shouldn't someone call the police?" she asked, since Hank seemed, for the moment at least, incapable of making decisions.

"Done," the off-duty police officer assigned to the production responded just as sirens began their nerve-racking whine a few blocks away. He was already trying to move people back from the door without letting them get too far out of sight. His partner was doing his best to establish a perimeter around an area meant to close in potential suspects and eliminate curiosity seekers.

With her own options quickly diminishing, Molly edged away from the two officers. She scanned the rapidly growing crowd, looking for Veronica, but there was no sign of the actress's glamorous attire amid the crew's denim and T-shirts. Surely the woman hadn't downed so many vodkas that she'd missed the sight of people streaming toward her trailer.

Torn between finding Veronica and calling her boss to report they were likely to be caught in the middle of a public relations nightmare, Molly prayed for a pay phone somewhere between the trailer and the outdoor café where she'd left Veronica. She could probably borrow a cellular phone from half the status-conscious people along the beachfront street, but that would mean having her conversation overheard by everyone who'd crowded around. There were also cellular phones galore in the production trailer, but the prospect of being inside that confined space with a murderer on the loose nearby made her stomach churn.

It hadn't been all that many months since she'd discovered a body in the card room of her own condominium. The murderer had later taken her hostage and left her to die in a sweltering storage shed. The claustrophobic memory was still spine-tinglingly fresh. She opted for a pay phone half a block away, searching for a quarter and Vince's home number in her purse.

The call to Vince elicited a stream of obscenities. Since she'd barely said "Hello," she guessed she'd caught him in the middle of his Saturday night seduction ritual. No wonder he'd insisted the number be used only in dire emergencies. The flow of invective and the rustle of sheets stopped abruptly when she casually mentioned the murder. That, at least temporarily, cooled his ardor. She'd always wondered what it would take.

"Murder!" Vince repeated. "What the hell are you talking about? What murder?"

"Actually, there's a slim possibility that it might be suicide," she said demurely. "But I wouldn't count on it."

"Molly, who exactly is dead and pr⌐
do you think they've been murdered?"

The determinedly patient note in Vince's vo⌐
suggested that he'd finally recognized just how close
she was to hysterics. Even her unobservant boss
could tell that she was really not happy about being
one of the two people to find Gregory Kinsey with a
bullet through his head.

"Molly? Are you there? Molly!"

She sighed. "I'm here. Gregory Kinsey's been
shot. He's dead. The police are on the way. That's
all I know."

"Shit!"

"My sentiments exactly."

"Who did it?"

"Vince, I've already told you the sum total of
everything I know. The murderer's name was not
included. Don't you ever listen?"

They both knew the answer to that. Vince's attention span was only slightly lengthier than a tod-
dler's in a toy store. Countless spurned women
could attest to that.

"Stay there," he said. "Whatever you do, do not
leave until you know exactly what's going on. If anyone from the media asks, issue some sort of statement. We regret, et cetera, et cetera. You know what
to say."

She noticed that Vince did not offer to leave his
comfortable bed to join her.

"I'll think of something," she said bleakly. She
couldn't imagine what. The movie's publicist would
probably have more than enough to say for all of

out. I wonder if all that glue has calories. I need to drop three pounds by next weekend, if I'm going to wear that slinky silver dress to that world hunger benefit performance."

"Liza!" If Molly didn't stop her now, Liza was likely to go off on some convoluted dissertation on world hunger. Her sharp tone apparently registered.

"Sorry," Liza said, immediately contrite. "What's the favor?"

"Brian is due home from his soccer game any minute and I can't get away from the film location. Can he stay at your place?"

"If he can lick stamps, he can stay. How's he getting home from soccer? Do I need to pick him up?"

"No. Michael or one of the parents is supposed to drop him off after they all go out for pizza."

"Michael, hmm?" Liza had taken an inordinate interest in Molly's relationship with the tall, dark, and handsome detective who'd investigated the murder in their Key Biscayne condo. The casual mention of his name had clearly placed her curiosity on full alert.

Hoping to forestall a lengthy interrogation, Molly warned, "Liza, I do not have time to discuss Michael O'Hara or my social life."

"Oh?" Liza said, all innocence. "I wasn't aware that you had a social life or that you could link such activity with Michael O'Hara in the same breath. Does that mean things have changed since I left for Guatemala last month?"

"It doesn't mean a damn thing, except that I am at my wits' end and I do not have time for this,"

Molly snapped, suspecting she was wasting her breath. Liza was not known for staying on track or taking a hint, no matter how directly or waspishly it was phrased.

"What's happening over there? Is it exciting? Maybe I should take a break from all this disgusting glue and bring Brian over to watch. I know it's late and all, but it's not a school night, right? Besides, I wouldn't mind getting a close look at Gregory Kinsey. From what I've seen he's quite a hunk."

"Not anymore," Molly mumbled.

"What?"

"He's dead."

There was an instant of stunned silence. Then, her tone suitably sober, Liza said, "Gregory Kinsey is dead? What happened? Molly, are you okay?"

Molly responded to the genuine note of caring in her friend's voice. "I'm as well as can be expected considering the fact that we are about to have police and reporters swarming all over the place, and I don't have answers for any of them. Not that the police are going to expect answers from me, but the reporters might, and if I don't have them, Vince will kill me."

"Molly, you're babbling."

"Don't you think I know that?" she retorted. "Liza, I've got to run. I have to get to Veronica. Greg's body was found in her trailer. I don't think she knows about it yet."

"Oh, my God. Do you suppose . . ."

Molly hung up without supposing a thing. She had to find the actress and warn her that all hell was about to break loose. Then she had to figure out how she could help to stem the tide of all the negative publicity.

Unfortunately, a survey of the outdoor café where she'd left the star less than twenty minutes earlier proved fruitless. Either Veronica was suspiciously aware of the fatal shooting in her trailer and had vamoosed to safer ground—Miami International Airport was a hub for all those tempting Latin American locations that didn't have extradition treaties. Or she'd gotten tired of waiting for her call and had simply gone back to her hotel in a snit. Either way, the police were not likely to be happy about the absence of a woman likely to be a prime suspect.

Rather than wasting time trying to guess how Veronica's mind worked, Molly skirted the crowd outside the murder scene and went back to the production trailer. The same people were gathered inside. Now, though, a palpable tension had replaced the boredom.

Hank Murdock, his usually affable expression grim, tried to pop open a soda, only to drop the can and send a dark spray all over the pale green carpet. No one moved to wipe it up. Hank just reached for another can. Jerry Shaw sat at the table and drummed his fingers in a nervous rhythm. Molly sat down beside him.

"You okay?" she asked.

He shot her a disbelieving look. "Do I look okay? The country's greatest film director since Hitchcock has just been murdered by a conniving bitch and you ask if I'm okay? Are you nuts, lady?"

Hank glared at him. "Shut up, Jerry."

Jerry's face crumpled. "Jesus," he murmured over and over. "Jesus."

"Did you find Veronica?" Hank asked Molly.

She shook her head. "There was no sign of her at the café. I was hoping she'd come back here. I doubt she ventured back to her own trailer with all that commotion outside."

Jerry muttered a cynical remark under his breath, but Molly chose to ignore it. "Maybe I should call the hotel," she said. "If she's back there, she should be told what's happened."

"As if she didn't know already," Jerry muttered darkly.

"I thought I told you to shut up," Hank said. "Taking pot shots at each other won't help anybody right now. We need Veronica if we're going to bring this film in, so watch what the hell you say to the police."

Molly stared at him. "You intend to finish the picture?"

The assistant director met her gaze evenly. "There's a helluva lot at stake here. Besides, it's what Greg would have wanted. We all owe it to him to pull together and see that his last film is a fitting tribute to his genius."

The sound of distinct clapping came from the trailer's open doorway. "I couldn't have said it better," producer Laura Crain said as she stepped inside. Her brown eyes were red-rimmed, but her narrow face was utterly composed.

Molly couldn't tear her gaze away from Laura's performance. Gossip on the set and in the tabloids had linked Laura and her boss romantically from the first day of production. The chemistry between Greg and the older producer had been obvious to anyone observing them in the same room for more than a few seconds at a time. The long, soulful glances, the steamy stolen kisses, the briefest of touches that occurred too often to be accidental.

From what Molly knew, Greg Kinsey never made a film without making a conquest in the process. Forty-year-old Laura Crain, with her stylishly cut frosted hair and nearsighted squint, had apparently been chosen as beneficiary of his affections on this production. Had the thin, hyperactive producer known that the romance was doomed to end in the next couple of weeks? Or had she, like all the others in his past, assumed she would be the one who lasted?

Whatever her emotional turmoil over Greg's death, Laura Crain wasn't about to let it show. She was quite possibly the best actress of them all, Molly decided, watching her move to Hank's side. With her clipboard in hand, she methodically went over a dozen scheduling details as if the murder had been no more than a minor glitch in an otherwise routine day.

Hank listened for several minutes, then gently placed a hand over hers. "Stop," he commanded softly. "There's not a damn thing we can do tonight and you know it, so you might as well give it up. Go tell the crew to start breaking for the night. They can get the equipment loaded. They might as well get a decent night's sleep, once the cops are through."

Laura stared at him helplessly, tears shimmering in her eyes. "But . . ."

Hank's gaze locked with hers. "It's okay, babe. You hear me? Everything is going to be okay."

A fresh batch of tears finally spilled down Laura's cheeks. Hank stood up and awkwardly pulled her into his arms. As Molly watched, Laura's shoulders shook with silent sobs.

Of all the people affiliated with the production, Molly had worked with Laura most closely, but she didn't feel she really knew her. Laura was one of those women who never seemed to relax around other women, as if she viewed them all as competition, no matter how farfetched that idea might be. Even so, Molly felt she had to say something to her now, offer some sort of consoling words.

She crossed the trailer. "Laura, I just want you to know how very sorry I am about Greg. I'm here to help you in any way I can."

Laura whirled on her, her eyes flashing furious sparks. "Help? It's because of you that this happened. Greg would be alive today, if you hadn't convinced him to bring this production to Miami. We could have shot it anywhere, but he told me how persuasive you were, how accommodating." Her voice turned even more spiteful as she added slyly, "I wonder exactly how accommodating you were."

"That's enough!" Hank said firmly to Laura, when Molly could only stand there gaping. He shot an apologetic look at her. "Molly, maybe you could go out and see what's happening. The sooner the police talk to all of us, the better. I need to call Duke

Lane at the hotel and tell him what's happened. Then I'll go talk to the crew about the schedule."

Since there was nothing to be gained by standing there defending herself against Laura's ridiculous accusation, Molly left.

Outside, the temperature remained in the mid-eighties. The breeze off the Atlantic barely stirred the muggy air. It was still preferable to being inside the trailer where the temperature and the atmosphere were both icy.

Molly found the off-duty officer still standing outside Veronica's trailer and introduced herself. "Who's in charge of the investigation?" she asked him.

"Sergeant Jenkins. He's inside."

"Any chance you can find out what sort of timetable he has in mind for questioning everyone?"

The officer was past being anxious to please, but still too much a rookie to know how to dismiss her with the haughty glance his superiors had perfected. "I'm not supposed to leave here," he said, rather than refusing outright.

Molly glanced from him to the door and back again. "I'd say you can take two steps, open the door and poke your head in. If you'd rather not, I could do it myself."

He decided there was less to lose by asking himself than giving her permission to venture inside. Molly'd been right. It took him exactly two steps to reach the door. After one swift glance to make sure Molly hadn't followed, he opened the door a discreet crack and called to the sergeant.

A minute later a tall black officer who looked as

if he'd played tackle for the Dolphins loomed in the doorway. He leaned down, listened intently, glanced at Molly, nodded, made a terse comment she couldn't hear, then shut the door. Firmly.

"He says he'll let you know when he's ready to take statements," the off-duty officer told her, an undeniable glint of satisfaction in his eyes. "Meantime, he says, don't go far."

"I wouldn't dream of it." She spotted an open table at the café across the street. "I'll be right over there, whenever he needs me." There wasn't a chance in hell that she'd go back to the trailer for another round with Laura Crain. She glanced back at the policeman. "If any reporters want a statement from my office, can you direct them across the street?"

He looked hesitant, but finally decided that wouldn't be breaking any of the rules drummed into him about crime-scene protocol. "I'll send 'em over. You might make out a list of everyone from the production company who was on the set tonight. It'll save Jenkins some time."

"I'll do what I can," she said, then walked back to the café and settled down to wait.

Apparently, Sergeant Otis Jenkins did not regard her as a primary witness. Nor did he seem all that interested in the list she had diligently prepared. Perhaps he'd merely decided to save the best for last. At any rate, by the time he finally got around to strolling across the street and joining Molly, she was awash in a sea of iced tea. It was a wonder she didn't slosh. Her nerves jangled from all the extra caffeine.

Sergeant Jenkins didn't waste a lot of time on preliminaries. Nor did he try to finesse any surprise answers from her. He merely announced that he'd already zeroed in on the killer. All he wanted were any of Molly's observations that might help him clinch the case.

Since catching a killer took time—unless he was foolhardy enough to stand around with a smoking gun still in his hand—Molly regarded the policeman skeptically.

"Was there an eyewitness?"

"Not to the shooting," he admitted.

"What, then? Fingerprints on the gun?"

"How about I ask the questions?"

"Ask away," Molly invited.

"Did you hear the argument between Gregory Kinsey and Veronica Weston?"

"I heard the noise, not the content," she said. With a sinking feeling in the pit of her stomach, Molly realized exactly where Otis Jenkins was heading—straight out on an obvious limb.

After the way he'd deliberately snubbed her earlier, she could hardly wait to saw it off.

CHAPTER
THREE

"I don't think there's any question about who's responsible," Sergeant Jenkins told Molly with a certain amount of grim satisfaction written all over his face. He resettled his bulky frame in the cramped plastic chair, trying to find a comfortable position. He finally gave up and perched on the edge of it.

"Given the timing, the fact that Kinsey and Veronica Weston were overheard arguing all day long, and the fact that he's lying on the floor of her trailer, it all adds up to one thing," he concluded, snapping his little black notebook shut.

Before he could say what that one thing was Molly stepped in to question his addition.

"Where's the murder weapon?" Molly interrupted as casually as if she were inquiring about the location of the Atlantic Ocean across the street. "Was it in the trailer?"

Jenkins looked slightly miffed, a surefire indicator that she'd hit on something that was equally troubling to him. "Don't worry. We'll find it. And when we do, I'm sure we'll find Veronica Weston's prints on it."

Even though she couldn't dismiss the fact that Veronica was every bit as absent as the gun used to kill Greg, Molly shook her head. She was absolutely certain of Veronica's innocence.

"I don't think so," she told the disgustingly smug detective. "Besides, all the killer would have to do is toss it in the canal along the MacArthur Causeway or take a midnight ride into the Atlantic and toss it overboard. Odds are you'll never find that gun. So much for means."

Jenkins cast a pleading glance heavenward. "God, I hate people who think they know everything just because they watch reruns of *Perry Mason*."

Molly scowled at him. "Forget Perry Mason. All it takes is a little common sense. It's pretty obvious you haven't got diddly beyond opportunity and, believe me, that's pretty shaky. What's Veronica's motive supposed to be? Gregory fought to give her this role. It was a break she badly needed. Why would she kill him in the middle of the production?"

His expression suggested he couldn't imagine why women did anything. He glossed over the problem. "Lady, by the time the night's over and we press charges, I guarantee we'll have means, motive, and opportunity pinned down."

To be sure she got the message, he ticked them off on his fingers. "If she came into town with a gun, we'll know it. If she bought one here, we'll find the record. There's your means. She was in that trailer. There's opportunity. The man was pushing her on the set, disregarding her opinions. I have half a dozen witnesses or more who'll swear in court that she hated the man's guts.''

"Having a professional disagreement hardly translates into hating his guts,'' Molly shot back. "Besides, what about the fact that he was still alive when she left the trailer?''

The words were out of her mouth before she even realized consciously that she actually was able to provide Veronica with a nearly airtight alibi. Greg had been alive when Veronica crossed that street! Suddenly there wasn't a doubt in her mind about that.

Just as suddenly, the detective's gaze was riveted on her. "How do you know that?''

Molly considered her answer carefully, trying to determine exactly why she was so certain. It went beyond mere intuition, though she never dismissed that either.

"Because I was sitting right here listening to them arguing,'' she told him finally. "You could hear them blocks away probably.''

Jenkins nodded. "That's what everyone's said. Like I said, the woman's guilty as sin.''

"No. He was still shouting when the door of the trailer slammed.''

As she described the moments before she and Jerry had discovered Greg's body, Molly tried to re-capture the exact sequence of events. Even as she described what she remembered, she had the feeling that she was missing one crucial detail, but for the life of her she couldn't recall what it was.

"The next thing I knew, Veronica was walking across the street," she told Jenkins. "She was with me every second until four, maybe five minutes before we discovered the body. Besides that, she was the one who sent me looking for Greg. Would a woman who'd just killed a man do that? Where'd she hide the gun? She wasn't carrying a purse and I guarantee that flimsy chiffon number she was wearing didn't have pockets suitable for concealing a peashooter, much less a firearm."

Sergeant Jenkins did not give up easily. "It's hard to say what any of us would do given the right circumstances or how cleverly we might be able to conceal something. Now, let me see if I have this right. You're claiming that Veronica Weston couldn't possibly have shot Kinsey because you were with her up until a few minutes before you found the body, right?"

"Exactly," she said, pleased that he'd caught on so quickly. Before he could remind her how many seconds were required to pull a trigger, she added, "And during those minutes I was a lot closer to her trailer than she was. I would have noticed if she'd gone back."

The detective's gaze narrowed. "How well did you know the victim?"

Molly was shaking her head before the question was out of his mouth. "Oh, no, you don't. You're not going to pin it on me. My job depends on keeping people like Gregory happy, not shooting them in cold blood, no matter how often I might want to.

And I happened to like Gregory Kinsey and his films.''

"No motive?'' he said, subtly mocking her.

"No motive,'' Molly concurred. "And for the record, no means. I don't own a gun and wouldn't have the foggiest idea how to shoot one.''

"I'm so relieved. I don't suppose you have any inside knowledge about someone who, in your educated opinion, does have a motive?''

Molly wished with all her heart that she had an answer for him, if only to wipe the smirk off his face. Unfortunately, she didn't. "No,'' she murmured reluctantly.

"Excuse me? I couldn't quite hear that.''

She glared at him. "No, I do not know who had a motive.''

"Thank you. You may go home now. We'll be in touch about having you make a formal statement.''

"Sorry. My boss has other ideas.''

He stood up and loomed over her. "Unless your boss is the president of the United States or maybe the governor of this state, it might be best if you remember that I'm in charge around here now.'' He waved a finger under her nose. "I've read about you, DeWitt. You were up to your earlobes in that case over on Key Biscayne a few months back. Nabbed yourself a few headlines, so now you think you know it all. Well, I don't want you messing in my territory. Got it?''

Molly decided she did not like Sergeant Otis Jenkins. She did not like his superior, mocking attitude. It was obvious he intended to make her job as difficult as possible. Maybe he thought it was fair

play, since she'd just shot a significant hole in his
case against Veronica.

"Sergeant, believe me, if I had any choice in the
matter, I would go home, pour myself a glass of
wine, and forget all about the events of the last couple of hours. However, like you, I am paid to be
here. I will try not to get in your way, but I will stay."

The masculine groan behind her registered
about the same time that the Miami Beach detective
deliberately turned his back on her. Since further
conversation with Jenkins appeared likely to be un-
productive, Molly turned and found herself face-to-
face with yet another police detective, one with
whom she'd become more or less intimately ac-
quainted when he'd investigated the murder in her
condo building.

As she met Michael O'Hara's resigned gaze, she
mustered a cheery smile. She could guess with some
accuracy what his reaction was likely to be to her
declaration. Cops, to a man, were reasonably predictable when it came to having outsiders play amateur sleuth. Mix that with Michael's instinctive Latin
machismo and mile-wide streak of protectiveness
and she had a pretty good idea of what was on his
mind.

"You heard?" she said, trying not to notice that
he looked every bit as gorgeous as the last time
she'd seen him. She'd had this wild hope that his
appeal would fade with time. It hadn't.

When he nodded, she said, "How much?"

"Enough to know that you're up to your pretty
neck in another murder investigation. Molly, take a

little advice. Do what the detective suggested. Go home. I will be happy to take you, in fact.''

She sighed. ''Believe me, I wish I could, but I can't. The film office is going to have to do everything in its power to counteract the bad publicity from Greg's murder. Vince insists that I stick around for every little detail.''

Michael grinned. ''Exactly how many details are you expecting to get from Miami Beach's finest law enforcement officers?''

Molly glanced at the stiff, retreating back of Sergeant Jenkins. ''Not many,'' she admitted. ''What are you doing here anyway?''

He shrugged in a lousy attempt at innocence. ''Hey, it's Saturday night. South Beach is hot. Even cops get a night off once in a while.''

Molly glanced around for some sign of his live-in lover, the sexy and volatile Bianca. As far as she knew, they were still together, despite his vague promises to end the relationship. He seemed to be alone. He was wearing faded jeans that hugged narrow hips and a knit shirt, not the kind of classy attire a man with Michael's elegant taste would choose for a night on the town. It didn't add up, especially since no more than an hour or two ago he'd been coaching a gang of eight- to ten-year-old soccer players way down in Kendall. Judging from the grass stains on the knees of his jeans, he hadn't gone home to change. She probed for a more truthful explanation.

''So as long as you were in the neighborhood, you thought you'd check out the latest hot murder scene?'' she said, her skepticism showing.

"You know how cops are," he said blandly. "We can't resist the lure of a dead body."

She shook her head. "Try again."

His grin was unrepentant. "Okay, you got me. I stopped by your apartment when I brought Brian home after the soccer game. Liza told me what had happened. She guessed you'd be in the thick of things. The three of us agreed that I'd come check things out and get you out of here."

"How democratic! Don't I get a vote?"

"It'd still be three to one. We win."

If she was prepared to be totally honest with herself, Molly had to admit that it had crossed her mind that Liza might tell Michael if the opportunity arose. She hadn't been at all certain what he would do with that information. As he was a Metro-Dade homicide detective, Miami Beach was not his jurisdiction. Nor was she his responsibility, for that matter.

Though she had seen Michael occasionally at Brian's soccer matches, more often than not Bianca was in the stands keeping a watchful eye on him. He'd been careful to maintain a polite distance from Molly in the months since he'd rescued her from that awful shed and solved the condo murder.

That hadn't stopped Molly from occasionally wanting to wrestle him to the floor and have her way with him. The man was sexy and elusive, a dangerous combination. Despite his past disclaimers, it was also clear to her that he was spoken for, which made him more dangerous yet. The fact that he was a memorable kisser added to the potential for fireworks. From her perspective the man represented nothing but trouble. Naturally, she was intrigued anyway.

Tonight, however, she was at least marginally more interested in his brain than in his body. He was a hotshot detective with an arrest-and-conviction record that was the envy of his peers and kept him on the good side of his superiors despite his troublesome tendency to question authority. Whatever his reasons for coming, Molly was very glad to see him. At times like these, it never hurt to have a staunch ally who knew the ins and outs of a murder investigation. She was not about to let him know that, though. A woman deserved to keep some secrets, after all.

Michael dropped into the chair just vacated by Sergeant Jenkins, waved her back into her own chair, and pinned her with that intense, brown-eyed gaze that had the ability to make the most reluctant witness spill his guts. It had an entirely different effect on her, but she was trying like the very dickens to ignore it.

"Fill me in," he suggested.

When he asked a question in that tone, she knew enough to cut to the bottom line. "Someone shot Gregory Kinsey in the head."

"Kinsey is?"

Molly regarded him incredulously. It frequently astonished her that not everyone followed the film industry as closely as she did. "He is . . ." She corrected herself: "He *was* one of the most talented new directors in Hollywood."

She listed his string of smash box-office hits. No sign of recognition flickered in Michael's eyes. She

had a hunch if she added Greg's list of female conquests, he might have better recall.

"How long's he been in town?" he asked.

"Production started the beginning of June. He
was here a week or so before that. He made one or
two trips prior to that to set things up."

"Not long enough to make any enemies, then?"

"None I'm aware of. He was a perfectionist,
which could set some people off, I suppose, but gen-
erally he was pretty easy to get along with."

"Into drugs?"

"Careful, Detective. You're guilty of stereotyp-
ing. All those Hollywood badasses do cocaine,
right?"

"Just covering all the bases. Drug deals gone
wrong account for a lot of untimely deaths around
here."

"Believe me, I'm no expert, but from what I saw
Greg was as straight as they come. The only things
that made him high were great lighting and a perfectly delivered line."

"Anybody blow their lines today?"

Molly scowled.

"Okay," he said without the faintest hint of regret, "let's assume for the sake of argument that the
killer is most likely someone connected with the
film. Has Kinsey been coming down hard on anyone
in particular?"

Molly was amazed at how quickly they fell into
their old routine of tossing around ideas and evidence. "I've gone over and over Greg's interaction
with every crew and cast member since the minute
they arrived on location. I haven't been on the set

every minute, but I think I have a pretty good idea of the dynamics.''

"And?"

"On the surface, every single person involved seemed to regard Greg with a certain amount of awe. When people had legitimate gripes, he listened. Once he made a decision, though, it was final and everyone knew it. Only Veronica dared to argue with him. Believe me, though, she could hold her own without resorting to shooting someone. Everyone connected with GK Productions had a vested interest in keeping Greg alive. As for Veronica, she had more to lose than anyone else if Greg didn't finish this picture.''

"Then why is this Veronica the one Jenkins is zeroing in on?"

"I don't think he is anymore, at least not exclusively. I tried to set him straight. Veronica was with me at the time Greg was shot. He was still alive when she left that trailer. I heard him shouting after she'd slammed the door and started across the street.''

"Then why'd she skip?"

"How do you know that?"

"They put out an APB on her while I was driving over here. Innocent people don't usually run.''

"Maybe she figured they'd blame her and got scared. Maybe she just got fed up with waiting and left before she even realized anything had happened. There's only one way to find out.''

Michael was shaking his head before she'd finished the sentence. "Oh, no.''

Molly was already on her feet. "Oh, yes. I'm going after Veronica. I have to warn her that the police are looking for her to question her.''

''If she's the killer, don't you think she'll have guessed that?''

''She is not the killer. How many times do I have to tell you that?''

''Until you can suggest a viable alternative,'' Michael retorted. ''Until then everyone connected with this production is a suspect. Including, I might add, you.''

''Oh, please.''

''Just stating the facts as Sergeant Jenkins is likely to view them. Despite whatever he said about presuming Veronica to be guilty, I'm sure he'll do a thorough investigation to rule out all the other candidates. In the meantime, don't you think you ought to get home to your worried son and distraught friend?''

Molly glowered at him. ''Brian will want all the gory details. As for Liza, the only thing she's distraught over this week is the decimation of the rain forest. If I get home too soon, she'll have me licking envelopes. You, too.''

''I'd rather lick a few envelopes than watch you get entangled in another murder investigation. Didn't you learn anything last time?''

Molly had to admit that Michael looked genuinely troubled by the prospect of her involvement. ''I didn't ask to be involved with this one. It happened. I'm here. I can't very well pretend everything's hunky-dory, can I?''

''You could,'' he said—a little wistfully, it seemed to Molly.

"But I won't." She could be every bit as bull-headed as Michael O'Hara. "I don't suppose you'd like to have a little chat with Sergeant Jenkins before we leave?"

"We?" he repeated, ignoring the rest. He, at least, knew better than to interfere in someone else's case.

"I can't imagine that you actually intend to let me go in search of Veronica on my own. I mean, I could sneak away when you're not looking, but being the outstanding detective that you are, you'd figure out in no time where I'd gone. Then you'd feel morally compelled to chase after me. Ergo, we might as well go together and save on mileage for the county."

A familiar, irksome expression of tolerant amusement spread across his face. "Since you're the only one on the clock, we'll take your car."

Once they were in her snappy white LeBaron convertible with the top down, Molly regarded him slyly. "What exactly would it take to get you officially involved in this case?"

"An act of God," he said. "Don't even think about it."

"Just curious," she said blithely. If she couldn't get him on the case officially, she'd just have to see that his curiosity was aroused. Veronica ought to be able to accomplish that without batting so much as an eyelash at him. At heart Michael was a man who just loved rescuing damsels in distress.

CHAPTER

FOUR

The hotel housing the cast and crew from the *Endless Tomorrows* production was one of the larger Art Deco structures facing the ocean. Its exterior was a brilliant white, trimmed in shades of turquoise and yellow. Elaborate bas-relief designs edged the doorway. A stucco railing, trimmed in the same pastel shades, curved around the porch that embraced two sides of the building.

At the moment that porch was crammed with enough reporters, photographers, and television cameras to intimidate anyone less determined than Molly was to enter the building. A harried hotel night manager, his balding head bathed in perspiration, was attempting to placate the hungry newshounds.

"Sorry," he said. "I cannot allow you inside. I must protect the privacy of our guests. You understand."

They obviously didn't understand anything except their own need for information. They pushed forward, backing him into the glass door. Another few minutes and he was likely to be as squashed as some bug on a windshield.

"Is Veronica Weston hiding out inside?" one aggressive TV reporter demanded, shoving a microphone toward the man.

"I really cannot answer your questions."

Molly pushed her way through the crowd until she reached the door. Michael was one step behind her. He leaned down and spoke quietly to the manager. Relief spread across the man's face. "Yes, yes, at once," he said, turning a key in the door.

Before they could enter, a reporter from the morning paper tugged Molly to one side. Though he looked as if he'd been awakened from a sound sleep and had grabbed the nearest rumpled shirt from the laundry basket, she recognized him from the mug shot that always ran with his Sunday column.

"You're with the film office, right?" Ted Ryan said. "Mrs. DeWitt?"

Molly nodded.

"Can you get me inside?"

"And have the rest of these guys accuse me of playing favorites? I don't think so. I'll try to get all of you whatever statements you need from anyone connected with the film. I can give you one myself on behalf of the film office."

"Fine. I'll take that at this point. I've got another twenty minutes to file. After that, anything I get will have to wait for the Monday paper. I'm ready to try climbing up the fire escape. I think my photographer's already halfway up to Veronica Weston's floor. Is she in there?"

"As far as I know."

"Are the police going to arrest her?"

At a warning glance from Michael, Molly modified her response to a politically correct "You'll have to ask the police that."

"What about you? What did you see at the scene? I hear she and Kinsey have been at each other's throats ever since shooting started. Any idea why?"

Molly shook her head. "Look, the only thing I can comment on for the record is that the film office will do everything in its power to cooperate with the authorities to see that the killer is identified and brought to justice."

"Come on," Ryan cajoled. "You can do better than that."

"Not and keep my job. Let me get inside and see if I can get someone from GK Productions down here to make a statement, okay?"

He motioned toward Michael. "What's he doing here? He's from Metro homicide. Is he on the case?"

Molly could just imagine the headlines: METRO CALLED IN TO BAIL OUT BEACH POLICE.

"No," she said hurriedly. "Absolutely not. Sergeant Jenkins is in charge."

"Then what's O'Hara doing here? It's his kind of case, isn't it? High profile. Politically sensitive."

Michael overheard the question and apparently guessed the direction of Ted Ryan's thoughts.

"Can't a guy go out with a pretty lady without you trying to make something of it?" he inquired lightly.

He stepped closer and slid an arm around Molly's waist to lend credence to his comment. Molly shot an incredulous look in his direction. She did not, however, pull away the way any sensible liberated woman might have under the circumstances.

Ryan looked skeptical, but he stepped aside to let them get into the hotel. "Make it snappy," he pleaded, glancing at his watch. "I'm desperate."

"Aren't we all," Molly muttered under her breath as she considered why she had permitted Michael to get away with such a sly innuendo about their relationship. Fortunately, she didn't have long to consider the implications. The elevator ride to Veronica's floor was mercifully short, allowing minimal time for introspection.

Veronica, wearing ice blue satin lounging pajamas with a plunging neckline, opened the door of her suite. She was clutching a tall tumbler of vodka. Molly could fully understand now exactly why Greg had cast her. She would fascinate any man old enough to distinguish between sexy glamour and the mere physical attractiveness of youth. It was pretty much like comparing rare vintage wine to grape juice. The source might be essentially the same, but only a fool thought they tasted alike.

The dazed expression on Michael's face told Molly he could fully appreciate the difference. Hooking him was going to be even easier than she had anticipated. What she hadn't counted on was this nearly uncontrollable urge she had to kick him.

"Veronica Weston, this is Michael O'Hara," Molly said.

At the mention of Michael's name, Veronica shot a disbelieving look at Molly. It was the same reaction most people had when trying to reconcile his dark-eyed, distinctly Hispanic appearance and faint accent with his Irish name.

As Molly understood it, the contradiction had to do with a vanished American father who left Cuba before discovering that his lover was pregnant. Michael's sentimental mother had given her son an Irish name in the man's honor. No one seemed quite sure if the father's name had actually been O'Hara, and no one, least of all Molly, knew with any certainty the impact this casual naming had had on shaping Michael's personality. Lord knew, he had the capacity for typically Latin machismo. The Irish influence was less easy to detect.

Right now, however, he was displaying a gentlemanly courtliness toward Veronica, who was suddenly radiating charm in sufficient kilowatts to light downtown Miami. The pair of them made Molly sick. Had everyone but her suddenly forgotten about the murder?

"Don't you think we should be concentrating on Greg?" she blurted finally, interrupting the flow of compliments Michael was directing toward the actress. Apparently he'd seen plenty of old movies, even if he was sorely behind the times on current filmmakers.

Both of them turned to look at Molly. Michael appeared slightly startled by her presence. Veronica looked irritated.

"Why on earth would I wish to discuss that imbecile?" she said, indicating a certain lack of respect for the dead or complete ignorance regarding his recent fate. Molly was so certain of the latter that she turned a look of triumph in Michael's direction. He was too much a cop not to take the hint.

"When did you leave the location?" he asked, slipping automatically into the interrogator's role he'd sworn not to take in this case.

Veronica answered without the slightest hint that she thought there was anything odd about the question or Michael's interest in the answer. "It must have been shortly after ten o'clock, wouldn't you say, Molly?"

"Later. It was nearly ten-thirty when you sent me to look for Greg."

Veronica nodded, sending her shoulder-length sweep of chestnut hair into sensuous motion. "Of course. I waited for some time and when neither you nor Greg came for me, I decided to call it a night."

"Was that before or after the police arrived?" Michael wanted to know.

"Police?"

Veronica managed a totally blank expression. It convinced Molly, but then she had to concede that they were dealing with a superb actress.

"You didn't hear the sirens?" Molly said.

"Who pays attention?" she said with an indifferent lift of one shoulder. "I spent months in New York, when I was doing that dreadful play on Broadway. Sirens blared all night long. I learned then to tune them out. What's this all about? Did something happen after I left?''

"Gregory Kinsey is dead," Molly said.

Veronica's eyes widened, and she took a long, slow drink of vodka, finishing off the last of it. She set the leaded crystal glass very carefully on the coffee table. Finally she swallowed hard, then looked directly into Molly's eyes.

"I don't believe it," she said convincingly. "How did it happen? I wasn't crazy about the man, but dead? He was so young." Without the glass to steady her hands, they fluttered nervously before she finally clasped them in her lap.

"Someone shot him," Michael said, his gaze pinned on her, obviously watching for signs of guilt.

"In your trailer," Molly added, so the actress would know exactly what she was up against.

Astonishment filled Veronica's eyes. "You don't think . . . Surely, you can't possibly . . ." She glanced from Molly to Michael and back again. "You do, don't you? You think I did it."

"I don't," Molly said stoutly. "I'm convinced it had to have happened while you were with me."

Veronica watched Michael, then asked, "Do you believe her?"

"It's not my case," Michael replied. "I'd have to say, though, that Molly does have pretty decent instincts when it comes to people. I think I know her well enough to say that I doubt she'd lie just to protect you. Unfortunately, her word may not be enough. From what I understand, there are a few minutes unaccounted for when Molly left you to go look for Greg."

"But I could see the trailer," Molly argued.

"The whole time? You told me you went inside the production trailer to ask for Kinsey."

She hadn't considered that as a flaw in her defense of Veronica, but she could see now that it might be. "That took thirty seconds, a minute tops," she argued. "That's hardly enough time for Veronica to leave the café, shoot Greg, and escape without me or anyone else seeing her. He had to have been killed before that, during the fifteen or so minutes Veronica and I were together. What I can't figure out is why no one heard a shot."

"With all that music blaring from every café on Ocean, I doubt you could hear a bomb drop over it," Michael reminded her.

"But . . ."

Veronica held up one perfectly manicured hand. "Molly, dear, if you will slow down for just one minute, I believe I can end all this absurd speculation about my role in Greg's death. I know for a fact that I was not the last person to see him alive, at least if we assume that your theory about the time period in which he was shot is accurate."

"What?" Michael and Molly said in unison.

"It's true. Just as I left the trailer Greg's latest conquest arrived. Surely you've seen her around the set, Molly. The tall, angular brunette with the kind of bone structure the camera loves. She doesn't speak much English, but I doubt Greg was interested in her conversational skills."

"Of course, that's it," Molly said as the elusive detail clicked into place. She had heard raised *voices* —plural, not just Greg's—even after she'd spotted

Veronica crossing the street. She hadn't readily linked the exchange to Greg because the shouts hadn't been in English. "She's Cuban, isn't she?"

"No. She's European," Veronica said with certainty.

"Italian, then?" To Molly's ear most of the Romance languages sounded pretty much the same at top volume. She understood Spanish only if someone spoke it very slowly and gestured at the same time. She'd taken French in school, which came in handy in Miami only when she had to deal with the occasional Canadian tourist or the Haitian immigrants whose Creole language owed its roots to French.

Veronica beamed. "Yes, of course. I remember now. She is a fashion model. She is here for a photo shoot for some European magazine. Greg met her at one of the cafés along Ocean Drive, two, maybe three days ago. You know how he falls in love with a gorgeous face. They've been inseparable ever since."

"I thought he was romancing Laura Crain," Molly said.

"Who's that?" Michael asked.

"The producer for the film. Greg was executive producer and director. Laura was the line producer. She handled the details with the studio in L.A. that's backing the film, saw to it that the budget was in line. She came here even before Greg to negotiate some of the contracts with the local unions, finalize housing for the cast and crew, that sort of thing. I worked with her quite a bit."

Michael nodded and turned back to Veronica. "Had Kinsey dumped her for this model?"

"I doubt it. The model was here only through tomorrow, according to what I heard. Greg probably intended to go right back to Laura the minute she'd gone. Besides, he was a very practical man. He wouldn't want his producer to take off before the movie wraps."

"Nice guy," Michael said. "Any idea what he and the Italian bombshell were arguing about?"

"No," Veronica said. "I was too furious with him myself to listen to the details of some contretemps between lovers."

Michael nodded slowly. "Okay. So he's got these two women on the hook. One of them we know had a fight with him tonight. The other might have discovered his fling and gone after him in a jealous rage. When Sergeant Jenkins gets here, I suggest you tell him everything you know about these two women. I don't suppose either of you knows the model's name?"

Molly and Veronica both shook their heads.

"Who's this Jenkins person?" Veronica asked, just as someone started pounding on the door of her suite.

"Police, Ms. Weston. Open up."

"That's Sergeant Jenkins," Molly said ruefully. "I don't suppose there's another way out of here."

Michael grinned at her as he went to the door. "Feeling guilty all of a sudden?"

"Something like that," Molly admitted, wishing he weren't opening the door quite so eagerly to admit the Miami Beach detective. "I did promise to stay out of his investigation."

"We all know what *that* promise is worth," Michael said.

Judging from the infuriated expression on Sergeant Jenkins's face when he realized who was in the room, she regretted she hadn't risked diving through a window.

• • •

Sergeant Jenkins looked more and more depressed as Molly and Veronica combined to shoot holes in his theory about the murder.

"So, you see, you ought to be out looking for that model," Molly concluded. "She was probably the last one to see Greg alive."

"Terrific. That's just great. I'm supposed to send people up and down Ocean Drive, maybe even along Collins Avenue, asking for an Italian model whose name we don't know. Do you know how many of these fashion things are going on over here at any one time?"

"Six last week," Molly retorted.

When he gaped at her certainty, she reminded him. "It's my job to keep track."

"And every one of those six shoots had dozens of models, right? Any other helpful suggestions?"

Molly shrugged. "Sorry. That's the best I can do."

The detective glanced over his notes. "What about this Duke Lane? He seems to be the only member of the cast who wasn't around tonight. How come?"

"He wasn't on call tonight," Veronica said.

"But he is your costar, right?"

"He has second-lead billing," Molly said quickly before Veronica could deliver one of her scathing comments about Duke Lane. "He should be around here, if you want to speak to him. Everyone was booked into this hotel."

Jenkins nodded. "I'll check before I leave. I assume I can count on all of you to come to me if you think of anything else that will help move this case along."

Molly nodded dutifully. Veronica and Michael were slightly more convincing with their replies. At least, the sergeant appeared satisfied.

As he opened the door to leave, a distinguished-looking man with a salt-and-pepper crewcut and clothes that looked as if they'd been bought on London's Savile Row hurried down the corridor. He spotted Veronica and held open his arms.

"Veronica, my dear, what is this terrible thing that's happened? They tell me Greg is dead. You must be devastated."

Before he could embrace the actress, Jenkins stepped into his path. "Who are you?" he inquired.

"Jeffrey Meyerson, Ms. Weston's fiancé."

Veronica appeared slightly nonplussed by the assertion, but she didn't deny the relationship. She merely looked the man in the eye and asked, "What are you doing here, Jeffrey? I thought you were flying to Rome this weekend."

"I intended to, but I thought I'd stop off and surprise you. Then when I saw Laura in the lobby and heard what had happened, I was doubly glad I did. Are you okay, my dear?"

"I'm fine," Veronica said, sounding incredibly sober and convincing for a woman who'd downed several double vodkas over the past few hours.

Despite Veronica's reassurances, Jeff Meyerson surveyed the trio of onlookers and suggested, "Perhaps, if you could leave us alone."

Jenkins looked disgruntled by the dismissal, despite the fact that he'd been on his way out the door not two minutes earlier. Michael nudged Molly toward the door as well.

"What's your hurry?" she grumbled as he tugged her along to the elevator.

"I want to get to a phone," he replied.

"Why didn't you just use the one in Veronica's room?"

"I didn't want Jeffrey Meyerson listening in."

"Why not?"

"Because the last flight from L.A. should have gotten in about three hours ago. Unless that flight was very late, it should have put him in town just in time to have murdered Greg Kinsey."

CHAPTER
FIVE

Molly tried not to gloat. She really did. But even though she knew she should leave well enough alone, the first words out of her mouth were, "I knew you couldn't resist."

Michael turned, his expression puzzled. "Resist what?" he asked. He didn't seem nearly as pleased as she was by the observation.

"Getting involved."

"I am not involved," he said emphatically. He jammed his hands into his pockets as if that would keep them from reaching for the phone again.

"Then why are you calling to check on flight schedules?"

He lowered the receiver of the pay phone back into place. "Instinct," he admitted. "But you're right. This is not my case. I'll find Jenkins and tell him what I suspect. Wait here."

Before Molly could protest, he'd stalked off

across the black-and-white hotel lobby that looked like a set from some thirties musical with Ginger Rogers and Fred Astaire.

"Well, damn," Molly muttered as she watched him disappear into the meeting room off the lobby where the police had apparently set up a temporary headquarters. This was not what she'd had in mind at all. Obviously, the hook hadn't sunk in deep enough. Michael had wriggled loose.

Thoroughly disgruntled, she walked over to the front door of the hotel, expecting to find the throng of reporters still lurking like seagulls awaiting a tasty catch. Instead, they had vanished, either satisfied by statements from the police or in search of more co-operative sources.

More likely, like Ryan's photographer, they'd headed for the fire escapes.

At any rate, outside it looked like any other Saturday night. Molly watched the endless parade of couples in attire that ranged from the downright eccentric to the most stylish available. As their conversation and laughter filtered through the glass, she tried again to sort through the various relationships she'd observed among the cast and crew on Greg's production.

Twenty-nine-year-old Duke Lane, of the slicked-back hair and bad breath, had been Laura's choice for leading man, from what Molly had read in the trades. His box-office following climbed with each new project. While Veronica's scathing assessment of the way he'd chosen to play the character of Rod Lukens was right on track in Molly's opinion, there was no arguing that he was giving a compelling, realistic performance. It was no doubt based on his own experiences. The man had an enthusiastically reported history of charming older women who could advance his career.

Still, if he hadn't been the director's first choice and if Veronica's complaining was beginning to get through to Greg, was it possible that Duke might have felt he had to kill the director? Molly dismissed the idea almost before it was fully formed. In that scenario, he'd probably have gone for Veronica. Besides, the picture was nearly complete. Greg would not have recast the role at this late date, no matter how he felt about Duke.

As for assistant director Hank Murdock, he'd get a directing break now that Greg was dead, but again, at this late date, how much good would it do him? *Endless Tomorrows* would always be regarded as Gregory Kinsey's last picture no matter who directed the final few scenes.

Production assistant Jerry Shaw didn't stand to gain anything from the director's death. To the contrary, he was barely out of the UCLA film program. He was riding quite happily on Greg's coattails.

Cinematographer Daniel Ortiz, who'd allegedly been busy setting up for the next scene at the time of the killing, owned a piece of GK Productions. The company's fate rested with the rise or fall of Greg's star. Molly would have to find out what would happen to GK Productions now that its primary owner was dead, but odds were it had a better future with him than without him. If so, the temperamental but talented Ortiz wouldn't want him dead.

All of which brought Molly right back to the women in the case. Again she dismissed Veronica as the least likely of the suspects. Laura Crain was Molly's first choice, if only because the producer had blindsided her earlier with that attack suggesting that Molly had used sex to lure Greg to Miami. There was also the jealousy motive to substantiate the choice. Laura might have sought revenge against the man who was publicly humiliating her.

As much as she wanted to pin it on Laura, however, Molly couldn't entirely dismiss the possibility that the mysterious model had ended her argument with Greg with a gunshot. Oh, how she'd like to find her before the police discovered her identity.

Just then she heard a commotion at the registration desk in the lobby. When she turned, she spotted a dark-haired, khaki-clad photographer, laden down with camera equipment, who was arguing with the clerk behind the counter. He hadn't come through the door since she'd been standing there, so she had to assume the man was checking out.

She listened to the exchange for several minutes before realizing that the two were arguing in a mix of English, Spanish, and a third language.

Italian! Of course! This had to be the photographer on location with Greg's model friend. As she had told Sergeant Jenkins, there were six crews currently shooting fashion layouts all over town, but only one that she knew of had an Italian photographer.

She inched closer to the desk, trying to detect

the man's name in the barrage of words being flung
back and forth. She finally gave that up as a lost
cause. They were talking so rapidly she couldn't
even distinguish one word from the next.

When tempers seemed to have cooled a bit, she
tapped the photographer on the shoulder. "Excuse
me."

He turned his still-stormy, intense gaze on her.
"Yes?" he said, immediately studying her with a
photographer's critical eye. Boredom followed rapidly. Molly didn't delude herself that she was model
material, but his relatively quick dismissal hurt.

She pulled one of her business cards from her
purse and handed it to him. "You are here from
Italy, aren't you?"

"Yes."

"Are you working with a particular model? Dark
hair. Dark eyes." Admittedly, it was a weak description given the likelihood that it applied to half the
models on location.

"I work with many models," he said carefully.
"Why do you ask this?" He studied her card more
closely. "You have work for one of my models?"

She considered a blatant lie, but settled for a
half-truth. "It's possible," she said. "Someone told
me this one is very beautiful. I'm in touch with a
number of casting directors who might be interested."

"Casting directors? These are from pictures?"

"Yes. We have a crew filming here now, GK Productions. Perhaps you've heard of them? Gregory
Kinsey? He's very famous."

His expression immediately closed down. He handed the card back to her with a disdainful glance.

"She would not be interested," he said, confirming her guesswork. She had the right photographer, and with any luck he could be persuaded to lead her to the right model.

"Perhaps I could ask her myself. What's her name?"

"She would not be interested," he repeated, then turned his back on her.

The reaction removed any lingering doubts that she had the right man. He clearly knew which model she meant, knew of her connection to Greg. And he was clearly protecting her, which must mean that he knew about the murder.

She moved to a more unobtrusive part of the lobby and watched as the photographer made a hurried call on one of the house phones. Then he gathered up his luggage and equipment and went outside, where a taxi was already waiting.

Molly nabbed a passing bellman. "Is there another way out of here besides that elevator?"

"The fire stairs. They come out on the alley in back."

"Damn," she muttered, racing through the door just in time to see the taxi turn into the alley.

She ran after it, cutting into the alley just as the taxi door slammed shut. It sped off in the opposite direction before she could get halfway down the alley. Cursing under her breath, she turned around and ran smack into Michael.

"What the hell do you think you're doing?" he demanded.

"Trying to stop Greg's model friend from skipping town before we find out what she knows about the murder."

He regarded her incredulously. "You found her?"

"I found the photographer she's been working for. Unfortunately, he figured out what I was up to and had her sneak down the stairs and come out of the hotel back here. I never even got a glimpse of her."

"Then what makes you so certain it was the right one?"

"Couldn't you, just for once, trust me? If I explain all that, they'll be halfway to Rome."

He ignored the sarcasm. "Any idea where they were headed?"

"Offhand, I'd say the airport. Isn't that where you'd go, if you wanted to leave town in a hurry?"

"Not at this hour. There are too few flights to choose from. I'd find some out-of-the-way hotel, hide out for a day or two, and then leave from Fort Lauderdale or West Palm Beach on a flight going somewhere other than Italy. I'd be a lot less conspicuous that way."

Molly shook her head. "Will I ever be able to think deviously enough to keep up with you?"

He grinned. "Is that a compliment?"

"Given the context, I'd have to say 'Yes.' Under ordinary conditions, however, it's not a particularly attractive trait."

"I'll try to use it judiciously."

She scowled at his teasing tone. "At any rate, the cab company ought to be able to tell us who's right."

"I don't suppose you got a glimpse of the taxi number or the license tag?"

"Actually, I did," she said. She repeated the digits, along with the name of the taxi company, which had its headquarters only a few blocks away.

"Then let's get back inside and give it to Sergeant Jenkins."

Molly tried to hide her disappointment and failed. "We're not going to track it down ourselves?"

"Not a chance, sweetheart. You've done enough amateur sleuthing for one night. We are going home."

"It would only take one little phone call. We'd turn the information over to the sergeant."

"The taxi company is not going to give that kind of information to anyone other than someone on official police business."

"You have a badge number, credentials, the whole nine yards," she reminded him. "You probably even have a contact there who'd like to do you a favor."

"But I am not the officer in charge of this case," he said with the pious tone of an altar boy wrongly accused of snitching a taste of wine. "I'm off duty, out of my jurisdiction. Are you getting the picture yet?"

"Yes," she said with a sigh. "What am I supposed to tell Vince? He expects me to handle things here."

"Tell him that the police have everything under control. Tell him that they hope to have the case wrapped up very quickly."

"Is that the truth? Or is that just meant to pacify him?"

"What do you think?"

"I think you've spent too much time around stonewalling public information officers. By the way, did Jenkins check on that flight from L.A.?"

"Better a little stonewalling, than a lot of wild speculation." He ignored the question about Jeffrey Meyerson's flight.

Molly gave up on that and tried to explain that facts tended to put a lid on speculation. She was so busy making her argument convincing that she barely noticed that Michael had steered her down the block and into her car.

"Give me five minutes," he said. "Then I'll take you home."

Obviously he had no idea what she could accomplish in five minutes if she put her mind to it. As soon as he'd left, she raced for the pay phone on the corner, dropped in a quarter, and called the taxi company.

"I'm calling from the hotel. One of our guests left something behind and I'm wondering if you could tell me where your driver dropped him off. The pickup was about five minutes ago, a couple. Italian. Giovanni, yes. That's it."

The dispatcher named an address in Little Havana. "That's a motel, I think," he added. Molly could visualize him leering as he said it. She was familiar with the name. Not far from the airport, the motel wasn't a stop-off for international travelers. Its usual clientele tended to rent by the hour.

Molly was back in her car, looking as innocent as it was possible for a guilty person to look, by the time he returned. He regarded her suspiciously.

"What's up?"

"Actually, I'm starving," she said. "I was hoping maybe we could stop for something to eat."

"We could just walk to the News Café. It's only a few blocks down."

"Actually, what I'd really like is a *medianoche* or a Cuban sandwich. Could we go to Versailles or someplace else over on Calle Ocho?"

"This sudden craving for Cuban food wouldn't have anything to do with a certain motel, would it?"

Molly felt her cheeks turning pink. "How did you know?"

"When Sergeant Jenkins called the taxi dispatcher, the man said he'd just had another call about the exact same couple. He said he'd told the woman they'd been dropped off at a motel in Little Havana."

"Oh," she said meekly. "I don't suppose . . ."

"No."

"But . . ."

"No." He glanced across at her. "Still hungry?"

"No," she muttered. "I'll drop you at your car on my way home."

He actually laughed out loud at that. "Not a chance. I won't rest easy until I know you're home and safely tucked in for the night."

"You planning to stick around for that?" she inquired testily.

His gaze caught hers and held. "Don't tempt me, Molly DeWitt," he warned softly. "Don't tempt me."

Awareness slammed through her and left her downright shaky. "How's Bianca?" she said in a desperate rush.

His eyes never left hers. "Fine," he said. "Last time I talked to her."

"You're not living together anymore?"

"No."

"I see," she said. "Whose choice?"

"It was mutual."

"I see."

His lips curved just slightly. "Do you really?"

Actually, what she saw with a flash of vivid insight was a night of pure, unadulterated lust and a morning filled with regrets. She toyed with the tantalizing prospect of ignoring her common sense, indulging in some hot, steamy sex, and simply dealing with the regrets when the time came.

Then she decided regretfully that she and Michael had skirted enough danger for one night. There were too many questions she wanted answered before she slept with a man who fascinated her the way Michael O'Hara did. Tonight she was too exhausted to ask a single one of them.

Since she feared that she'd murmur something incriminating if she opened her mouth at all, she remained silent for the rest of the drive back to Key Biscayne.

"You going to invite me up?" Michael inquired as they pulled into the driveway at the Ocean Manor condominium. His tone was casual, but the look in his eyes was anything but.

"Not tonight," she said finally.

"Too bad," he said, still keeping it light. "I was going to tell you what Sergeant Jenkins found when he checked the airlines about flights from L.A."

Molly chuckled at the deliberately devious ploy. "You can tell me that right here."

He shook his head. "I think I'll save it for breakfast."

"Breakfast?"

"I'll pick you up at ten."

"That's not breakfast. That's brunch, especially with an eight-year-old boy in the house."

"Give Brian a bowl of cereal to tide him over until I get here. I usually refuse to budge before nine thirty on my day off. I'm making an exception for you."

"Oh, in that case, I suppose I should be suitably grateful."

He leaned over and pressed a quick kiss against her lips. He was there and gone before the gesture had time to set off sparks. "Don't tax yourself. Just try to stay out of trouble until I see you again."

"I'll do my best," she promised. She had a feeling she'd already dodged the worst of it. A seductive Michael O'Hara—an apparently available Michael O'Hara—represented trouble with a capital *T* to most any woman past puberty. To one who'd clung to celibacy as fervently as Molly had ever since her divorce, he lured like those sirens who beckoned ships to their doom.

Even so, she couldn't help wondering what it would be like to court disaster.

CHAPTER
SIX

It wasn't until she was upstairs that Molly realized how cleverly Michael had stranded her right where he wanted her—far from the scene of the crime. If she hadn't been quite so exhausted, she might have dragged Liza out to chase after the sneaky detective who'd left her with nothing to drive. She wondered what would happen if she called the police to report that he'd made off with *her* car.

So much for the chance to race back to Miami Beach to do a little more sleuthing. There were plenty of people she hadn't really talked to after the discovery of Greg's body, beginning with the film's somewhat enigmatic director of photography, Daniel Ortiz.

Sternly reminding herself what curiosity did to that ill-fated cat, she checked her answering machine for messages instead. There were half a dozen from Vince, all self-described as urgent, and one from Liza telling her that Brian was sound asleep in her guest room and that he might as well stay the night.

"I, however, am waiting up for you," Liza's taped message reported. "I want to hear everything the minute you get home and I do mean *everything*, including how you're getting along with the hunk. Whoops! Probably shouldn't have said that. He could be there listening. Sorry. See you."

Molly chuckled at Liza's belated sense of discretion. She started for the door, only to hear the key turning in the lock. Obviously, Liza had heard her come in and hadn't trusted her to stop by and fill her in.

"Hey, there. It's me," Liza called from the doorway. "You alone?"

"What if I weren't?" Molly said. "It'd be too late now."

"True, but nothing shocks me anymore, and I'm a specialist at hasty exits."

"Right. Like the time you got out of Spain one step ahead of that bullfighter who took a fancy to your . . ."

"Never mind what he took a fancy to," Liza said, curling up on a corner of the sofa and tucking her bare feet under her. Her moussed, flattop hairstyle gave her the look of an innocent pixie, but the expression in her eyes was every bit as intent as Michael's in mid-interrogation.

"Okay, tell me what happened," she demanded. "Who killed Greg Kinsey?"

"About the only thing I can say with certainty is that it wasn't me," Molly told her from the kitchen.

She poured them each a glass of wine before joining Liza.

"Is Michael working on the case?"

"Officially, no, but he can't resist checking out clues any more than I can. Thanks for sending him over, by the way."

"*Sending him?* Are you kidding? I mentioned murder and the man flew out of here. I barely had time to tell him where you were. God, I love all that macho protectiveness."

"I told you, he can't resist a good homicide investigation. It doesn't have anything to do with me," Molly said, deciding Liza did not need to know just yet that Michael had all but invited himself into her bed tonight.

"Right. The man decided to spend his one night off chasing a killer who's not even in his jurisdiction. I'm telling you, Michael O'Hara would not have gone anywhere near Miami Beach tonight if you hadn't been involved."

Molly couldn't stop a wistful, unliberated sigh. "I have to admit I was glad to see him. It's as if whichever side of my brain is supposed to do deductive reasoning goes into high gear the minute he's around."

"To say nothing of your hormones."

"Okay. That, too."

Liza drank the last of her wine and stood up. "You look beat. Since you can't offer me anything juicier than speculation, I'm going home. I'll send Brian over in the morning."

"Just make sure he's back here before ten. Michael's picking us up for brunch."

"Oh, really? Maybe I'm getting out too soon after all. Isn't there some other little detail you'd like
to share with your best friend?"

"Wipe that smirk off your face. There are no
details," Molly retorted. "I'm going to bed. Let
yourself out."

As it turned out, going to bed was achieved far
more easily than getting to sleep. She kept remem-
bering the sight of Greg Kinsey lying dead and the
sound of the heated argument that had preceded it
by what must have been no more than minutes.

• • •

"Tell me about Kinsey," Michael suggested midway
through brunch the next morning, after he and
Brian had filled Molly in on every detail of the soccer game she'd missed. Her son beamed as Michael
lavished praise on a shot he'd made. She knew how
he felt. She wouldn't mind basking in a little of Michael's admiration.

Michael had arrived precisely at ten, wearing
perfectly pressed navy blue slacks, a pale blue dress
shirt with the sleeves rolled up to his elbows, and an
expensive gold watch no thicker than the very masculine hairs that subtly shadowed his arms. Lord,
the man was sexy, Molly had thought then and
thought again now. What had possessed her to send
him away the night before?

At the sound of Michael's chuckle, she blinked
and stared. "What?" she said blankly. Regretfully,
she forced her gaze away from his hands and her
attention away from the decidedly wayward thoughts
about what those hands could have been doing to

her during her long, sleepless night if she hadn't had an attack of conscience. Or cowardice. Probably the latter, she decided with a sigh.

A knowing twinkle sparked in his dark brown eyes. "Kinsey," he reminded her. "Tell me what he was like."

"You mean when she found his body with the bullet hole in the middle of his forehead?" Brian asked hopefully. At eight he was fascinated with anything that made Molly squeamish. The more gore, the better.

"No, I mean when he was alive," Michael told him, barely hiding a grin. "I pretty much know what dead guys are like."

Brian looked disgusted. "If you guys are gonna talk about all that boring stuff, can I go play on the beach?" he asked. "I finished eating a long time ago."

"Go," Molly said. "You know the rules. Stay within sight and don't go in the water."

"And be careful crossing the street," Michael added, glancing toward Ocean Drive's parade of convertibles and open Jeeps filled with teens and practically shaking with the sounds of rock. "The traffic's bumper-to-bumper."

When Brian had successfully navigated the street in front of the outdoor café, Molly considered Michael's question about Greg.

"He was driven," she said finally. "I've never met anyone so totally absorbed in what he was doing. He seemed to have this vision of what a scene should look like on screen, how it should be played. More important, he knew how to communicate that vision to those around him. I think everyone on the picture was really psyched about working with him."

"Had all of them worked with him before?"

"I think most of the crew had. I'm not so sure about the actors. I know this was the first time he'd worked with Duke Lane. Laura had insisted on casting him, and Greg respected her judgment when it came to box-office decisions."

"Why was she so anxious to get this Lane in the picture? Isn't he one of those hunk-of-the-month types?"

"Pretty much," Molly agreed. "But unlike some of the others, he can act. That was critical to Greg. He would never have agreed otherwise, I'm sure."

"Was this Laura more interested in his acting or his body?"

"Duke and Laura?" She tried to envision it and shook her head. "I don't think so."

"Okay, what about the others? Was Veronica someone Greg had used in other movies?"

"No, and that's what was so odd about him choosing her for this role. No one, from Laura to Hank to the production assistant, thought he should take a chance on her."

"Why? She has an incredible track record."

"*Had* an incredible track record," Molly corrected. "Her last couple of films were disasters, primarily because of her drinking. Supposedly she's gotten herself straightened out, but until Greg came along no one wanted to risk another overbudget debacle. She delayed her last film by nearly a month while she sobered up enough to shoot the final scenes."

Michael regarded her doubtfully. "Wasn't that vodka she was swilling down like water last night?"

"It was."

"Looks to me like she not only fell off the wagon, but is headed for a crash landing."

"I know. I don't think she was drinking when production started, though. In fact, I'd swear she was stone-cold sober every time I was on the set."

"When did that start to change?"

Molly thought back to the first time she realized Veronica had started substituting vodka for her bottled mineral water. "A week ago, maybe less."

"When did the fights with Kinsey start? About the same time?"

"Oh, no. She and Greg started battling on the first day of production. I've never seen two people go at it the way they have, especially two people with no past history."

"You're sure there's no past history there?"

"Not according to anyone I've talked to, and that includes Greg and Veronica. The tension on the set was beginning to take its toll. Yesterday, between that and the heat, everyone was snapping."

"What were the fights about?"

"The script and Duke Lane. Veronica wasn't wild about either one of them, and she was not shy about expressing her opinion. The writer, a newcomer named Jonathan Fine, has hidden out in his hotel room since the first day of production. She humiliated him in front of everyone. Greg had to talk him into staying around to make any script changes he needed."

"And Duke?"

"Duke steered clear of the set whenever he could. I have to give him credit. He never let her attitude get to him, at least not in public." She looked up just then and caught sight of the actor waiting for a table. "Speak of the devil."

Michael followed her gaze. With his eyes hidden by sunglasses, Molly couldn't see his reaction, but his surprised tone said it all. "That's Lane?"

"Yes."

"I thought he'd be . . ." Apparently words failed him.

"Taller? Sexier?"

"More imposing," Michael countered, which was a nice way of saying that Duke Lane wasn't exactly ready to do health club ads. Molly had had the same initial reaction. On-screen he had a larger-than-life presence. In person, with his slight frame and five-feet-seven-inch height, he was unimpressive, as ordinary as the boy next door.

Until he smiled. Then any woman would be able to say exactly what all the excitement was about. That smile combined a boyish eagerness to please and sleepy sensuality in a way that invited thoughts of wild sexual adventures. The glint in his eyes promised intelligence and fun. Molly had discovered that the expression didn't lie. Duke Lane was both smart and witty, facts too often lost in the Hollywood hype. She wanted Michael to see that side of him.

"Think we should ask him to join us?"

Michael gave her a wry look. "Could I stop you?"

"Admit it," she said. "You're every bit as curious as I am."

He leaned back in his chair. "True. Bring him on."

Molly stood up and walked over to the young actor, who was wearing faded jeans, a T-shirt, and cowboy boots. It was the same laid-back clothing style affected by his character Rod Lukens, the dressed-up boy-toy of the film. Either he liked to stay in character or he didn't waste his millions on wardrobe.

"Duke?"

He turned toward her and the famous Duke Lane grin spread across his face. "Molly! What a relief! I hate going out by myself. Some chick spots me and the next thing I know I'm mobbed. If I'd had one more hamburger from room service, though, I think I would have thrown up."

A pleasant image, Molly thought. "I'm with a friend. Come join us."

She led the way back to the table and made the introductions. She neglected to mention that Michael was a cop. Since he wasn't here in any official capacity, she figured it wasn't relevant. Interestingly enough, he didn't offer the information himself.

With a slight wave of his hand, Duke was able to get the attention of a waitress who'd been ignoring them since the instant she realized Michael wasn't interested. She sashayed over so fast she stirred a breeze that sent napkins from half a dozen tables fluttering to the ground.

Despite his claim that he craved anonymity, Duke removed his sunglasses and directed his baby blue eyes straight at the waitress, practically commanding her to recognize him. She didn't fail him. Her own eyes widened and her pencil dropped to the ground. Michael retrieved it since she seemed too busy staring in openmouthed adoration.

"You're Duke Lane," she said finally. "Ohmigosh. Wait'll I tell the others. Oh, wow!"

"What's good, honey?" His tone suggested he was interested in more than what was on the menu.

"Salads," she said in a breathy voice that indicated she had fallen victim to his sexy innuendoes. "We have *really* good salads."

Duke seemed to tire of the game. "Then bring me one," he said abruptly. "Dressing on the side. A bottle of mineral water." He winked at her. "We'll talk about dessert later."

Molly noticed that Michael was watching the entire act as if he ought to be taking notes. She felt like reassuring him that his own technique was considerably more effective, at least on any female over twenty-one.

"Terrible about Greg," Duke said when the waitress had left. "I had the car radio on and I heard it on a newsbreak. I almost crashed into a guard rail."

"What time was it on?" Molly asked, relieved that Duke had brought the subject up himself. "I didn't even think to see what time the story broke on the news."

"Midnight, maybe later. I was coming back to the hotel from having drinks with a friend down in Coconut Grove, some yuppie bar. Man, you ever go there on a Saturday night? That place is overrun with kids. I've never seen so many convertibles and boom boxes in one place before, except maybe Santa Monica beach in the summer."

"Any thoughts about who might have shot Kinsey?" Michael asked.

Duke frowned. "Who shot him? You mean it wasn't some kind of mugging or something? They didn't give any details on the radio. They just said he was dead."

Molly shook her head. "We were still on location. His body was found in Veronica's trailer."

The actor looked genuinely shocked. "Oh, man, you're kidding me. I know those two fought like jealous ex-lovers or something, but I didn't think she'd pull a gun and shoot him."

"So you think she did it?" Michael said, pouncing on Duke's comment.

Duke looked confused. "But you-all just said . . . He was in her trailer. I just assumed."

"Veronica has an alibi," Molly said staunchly. Michael looked unconvinced. So did Duke.

"You checked it out?" Duke said.

"I didn't have to. I'm her alibi, at least for all but a minute or two."

"No kidding. Then your guess is as good as mine. Everyone else loved Greg."

"Including you?" Michael inquired mildly, managing to sound as if his interest was only that of a casual bystander.

Duke turned his most sincere gaze on Michael. "Including me," he said emphatically. "I know he didn't want me on this picture. Hell, I know what half the serious directors in Hollywood think of me.

They think I'm a no-talent hotshot who's trying to capitalize on my looks."

He leaned forward, his expression intent. "Well, you ask any director who's actually worked with me and you'll get a different story. I know what the hell I'm doing in front of a camera. That's why the audiences want to see me, not because I've got some killer smile and a decent body. Those don't mean shit if you can't deliver your lines. Too bad Greg's not alive to tell you what I'm saying is true. We talked plenty over the last couple of weeks and the man respected me. I turned his attitude around and, believe me, it didn't happen because I could smile."

Duke leaned back in his chair, his arms crossed over his chest. His belligerent expression dared them to challenge him.

Michael met his gaze evenly, then finally nodded. "Okay, so you and Kinsey got along in the end. Somebody on the set didn't get along with him quite as well. Did you ever hear anything, see anything that looked like maybe somebody might not be as enchanted?"

"Besides Veronica, nobody. I flat-out don't believe there's a person involved with this production who could have killed him."

"You know anything about his personal life?" Michael asked.

To Molly's amazement, Duke didn't seem thrown by Michael's persistence. He answered readily.

"Nope. What the man did on his own time was

none of my business. I was too busy keeping my own squeeze happy to worry about his."

"Is your *squeeze* involved with the production?" Michael seemed to stumble over the description a bit.

"What difference does that make?"

"If she's been around, maybe she noticed something."

Duke hesitated for a split second before responding. "She's been around town, not around the set. Moviemaking bores her to tears."

Molly regarded him oddly. She tried to recall seeing Duke with a woman at any time since he'd arrived. She honestly couldn't remember a single occasion. He showed up, played his scenes, then retreated to the privacy of his trailer or went back to the hotel.

"Has she been here all along?" she asked cautiously. Apparently something in her tone alerted Michael that she wasn't entirely buying Duke's story. He turned his most penetrating gaze on Duke.

"From day one," the actor assured them both.

"Where is she now?"

"Asleep. Daylight's not her gig."

"Did you talk with the police last night?"

"I got a message they were looking for me, but we crashed when we got back to the room. I'll check in this morning."

Just then a car cruised to a stop right in front of them and Sergeant Jenkins emerged. He scowled at Molly and Michael. "You two are a long way from home, aren't you?"

"Just out for a pleasant brunch," Molly said cheerfully. "Care to join us?"

He looked at Duke Lane for several seconds before recognition sparked in his eyes. "Maybe I will at that." He waved his driver on, then stepped on the curb. He grabbed a chair from the next table, and wedged it between Molly and Duke.

"Duke Lane, right?"

"Yes."

"Sergeant Jenkins, homicide. Didn't you get my messages?"

"We were just talking about that. I figured I'd check in as soon as I got back to the hotel."

Jenkins glared at him. "Some police officers might view that attitude as uncooperative."

Duke shrugged. "Everybody's got hang-ups. Me, I'm the most cooperative guy you'll ever want to meet, once I've had my morning coffee. Before that, I can be real mean."

Jenkins glanced pointedly at the coffee cup. "Drink up. Then you and I are going down to headquarters for a friendly little chat."

Molly tried to hide her disappointment. She'd been hoping he'd go over Duke's story right here and now. Maybe he'd get an answer to the question uppermost in her mind.

Why the hell would Duke be lying about some woman when everyone on the set and in Hollywood knew he was gay?

CHAPTER
SEVEN

"What was that all about?" Michael asked Molly the instant Otis Jenkins and Duke Lane left for the police station.

"What was what all about?"

"Don't you dare play dumb with me," he chided. "Your eyes will give you away every time. You picked up on something. What was it?"

When he was regarding her with that intent, dare-you-to-lie cop look, Molly found it virtually impossible to skimp on the truth, even when she wanted to. "All that talk about Duke's squeeze," she admitted. "I've never once seen him with a woman."

"So he's discreet. So what?"

"He's not only discreet. He's gay."

Michael looked as if she'd just announced that cows flew. "Him? No way. Didn't you see the way that waitress reacted to him? I think she slipped him her phone number on one of those little napkins she dropped in his lap.''

Molly shook her head. "You saw what you expected to see when some heartthrob is out in public. Forget the way *she* reacted to him. Think about the way he reacted to her. He played the role to get her attention, but he never once looked her over."

Michael nodded as comprehension slowly dawned. "Okay, say you're right."

"I am right."

"*Say* you're right," he repeated with careful patience. "What possible difference does it make as far as Greg's murder is concerned?"

That stymied Molly as well, which was why she hadn't particularly wanted to bring it up. "If he'd lie about one thing, why not another?" she ventured.

"Maybe. Or just maybe he had a crush on the director."

"If he did, it was definitely unrequited. Greg's list of conquests, *female conquests,* was endless. To hear some of the guys tell it, he couldn't keep his pants zipped."

Michael's brows rose. "Exactly what do you and the boys discuss in your spare time?"

"They don't necessarily say things like that to me. They just say 'em when I'm around."

"Fascinating," he said, sounding oddly disgruntled. "If Greg wasn't gay, then Duke Lane's sexual preferences probably don't matter."

"Unless he propositioned Greg anyway and Greg shot him down."

"That's a stretch. You couldn't build a case

around something as speculative as that, not without witnesses.''

"At this point, I don't see much we can build a case around. I'm grasping at straws here. Help me out. You're the hotshot detective.''

Michael opened his mouth, but Molly cut him off. "And if you dare tell me to leave it to the Miami Beach police, I'll scream.''

"I wouldn't dream of it.''

"Good.''

"There is something I would like to know, though." At her nod, he said, "Why is it that you are constitutionally unable to leave well enough alone? I could understand it when it was your condo president and we thought the murder weapon belonged to you. But this time? I don't get it. This kind of idle curiosity can get you killed.''

"It's hardly idle curiosity. I was assigned to keep things running smoothly for this production. Instead, the director winds up dead. You've met Vince. If you were me, would you want to go to work tomorrow morning without some answers?''

"Molly, the man can't hold you accountable if some lunatic pulls a gun and shoots someone.''

"Vince can and, believe me, he will. Especially if he happens to get half a dozen calls from county officials wanting to know how the hell he could have allowed this to happen? He is more than willing to throw the burden of answering that question off on me. Surely you've dealt with the occasional boss who survives by passing the buck.''

From Michael's expression, she could tell that he had.

"True," he said. "Okay, let's make a deal, then. If you have a theory about what happened, you'll tell me about it and let me do some unofficial snooping. If you find something concrete, you'll tell Sergeant Jenkins at once and let him check it out. You will not stick your own neck out. Deal?"

With those brown eyes pinning her in place, Molly would have made a deal to sell her soul. "Yes," she said finally. "I promise."

Even as she said the words, she had a feeling they were likely to have about as much substance as her wedding vows. She'd meant them heart and soul at the time, but after a while they had lost their meaning.

The apt comparison came up again an hour later, when she and Michael left the elevator in her condo just in time to run smack into her ex-husband, who was prowling the hallway outside her apartment. Hal DeWitt ruined his good looks by glaring at her. He was obviously in a foul temper.

"Where's Brian? I'm taking him home with me," he announced without so much as a by-your-leave.

"He's outside and no, you are not taking him anywhere," she retorted, glaring right back at him. The man always brought out the worst in her. Since he often chose to ignore his son unless he could use Brian to gall her, she had no doubt about his motive in showing up today. He'd read about the murder and decided she was once again endangering his child.

"I won't allow him to live with a woman who's a damned jinx."

"Jinx," she repeated incredulously, her voice climbing.

"Two men are dead," he reminded her, a stubborn, accusing set to his jaw.

"Not because of me, they're not."

Since he couldn't win that argument, he directed a scathing glance at Michael. "Who's he?"

She made the introductions warily, watching as Michael seemed to sum Hal up with a quick once-over. Hal was still a very good-looking man, obsessive about staying trim and keeping a year-round tan despite the well-publicized risk of skin cancer. Unfortunately, he was well aware of his attractiveness. He'd skated through life on little more than his charm and his easy smile. Both were wearing thin, along with his carefully styled dark hair, which no longer quite covered his receding hairline.

Given a little time and vastly improved objectivity, Molly had finally come to see Hal DeWitt for what he was—a shallow, vain man who took delight in belittling everyone around him. His cutting remarks no longer had the power to hurt her. That didn't stop him from making them, however.

He waved the local section of the Sunday paper in front of her. "Just look at this! There you are, smack in the middle of another murder, your picture on page one. Don't you give a damn what your son thinks of you?"

Molly could practically feel Michael tense beside her. He took a protective step closer.

"Brian seems to think his mother is a very special woman. I'd say he's got it nailed," he said to Hal. His voice was deceptively mild.

Hal's face reddened. "This is none of your business. We're talking about my son."

Michael stepped toward her ex-husband, but Molly put her hand on his arm to stop him from defending her. She was getting better all the time at standing up for herself. Lord knew, Hal gave her enough practice.

"He's my son, too, and don't you ever forget it!" she reminded Hal coldly. "If you want to come inside and discuss this rationally, fine. If not, you can leave."

"If I leave, I'm taking Brian with me."

"No," she said with icy calm. "He will spend next weekend with you as scheduled, but he will not leave here with you today. I will not have his life disrupted because of your whims. If you so much as think of violating our custody agreement, I'll have you arrested and charged with kidnapping."

"And I will be only too happy to make the arrest," Michael offered.

Hal's expression turned mean. "This is between my wife and me."

"Your ex-wife," Molly corrected. "And as far as Michael's willingness to haul you off to jail, I will be only too thrilled to accept his help—" she regarded Hal meaningfully—"if it comes to that."

Few people ever talked to Hal DeWitt that way, and up until recently Molly had been no exception. He seemed stunned by the change in her. Sometimes, she thought wryly as she waited for his decision, she was every bit as startled as he was. Sparring with Michael had sharpened not only her wits but her self-esteem. *He* took her opinions seriously, something her husband had never done.

Whatever cockiness Hal had been feeling visibly drained right out of him. He salvaged some tiny measure of dignity by stalking off to the elevator without another word.

When he'd gone, Michael looked as if he were sorry he hadn't had the chance to throw a punch. Hal often made Molly feel that way as well.

"Do you think we ought to go down and make sure he leaves without taking Brian?" he said.

Molly shook her head. "The last thing he wants is to be labeled a kidnapper. He'd rather act the martyr. He'll get a lot of mileage out of that."

"How long did you stay married to the guy?"

"About six years too long. I should have left when Brian was a baby, but I thought he ought to have a father, even if I had to put up with a lousy husband. I figured I only got what I deserved. Then one day, not all that long ago, I might add, I woke up to the fact that I was a pretty decent, capable woman and I stopped doing mea culpas over robbing my son of a dad. I don't do anything to stand in the way of Hal and Brian having a relationship. I've never said one harsh word to Brian about his father and I hope I never will."

"Staying quiet must test your willpower."

"Oh, there are days," she admitted. "It's funny, though. I think Brian's figured Hal's shortcomings out for himself. No doubt one of these days Hal will blame me for that too."

"Maybe he'll just wake up eventually and realize

he ought to be damned proud of having such a savvy kid.''

Molly chuckled. ''I'm afraid you're crediting Hal with the ability to handle more introspection than he's capable of. The man doesn't mind gazing in the mirror, but he doesn't waste a second trying to understand what's in his heart.''

He studied her with obvious concern. ''You okay with what went on just now?''

''I'll survive.''

''I could stay.''

As tempting as the idea sounded, Molly shook her head. She wasn't going to turn to Michael out of loneliness and need. Whenever they finally got around to changing the nature of their relationship into something more intimate, it would be because the timing and the motives were right for both of them.

Michael took a step closer and Molly found herself backing up against the wall. Her breath snagged in her throat as he braced one arm on each side of her. ''We have some unfinished business between us,'' he said, brushing a stray strand of hair away from her face. His fingertips skimmed her cheek. ''One of these days we're going to have to take care of it.''

Molly's mouth seemed to go dry. As she moistened her lips with her tongue, Michael's gaze never left her mouth. Finally, when the tension between them was tightrope taut, he bent his head and slanted his mouth over hers. Instead of taking, though, as Hal had always done, Michael seemed to be giving her strength, filling her with something unfamiliar. It felt tantalizingly like joy, bursting inside with the radiance of sunbeams.

On the other hand, it might have been pure, unadulterated lust. It was impossible to think straight with all that hard, male sexiness and heat pressed against her. One more dizzying second and she was likely to forget all those commonsense warnings.

"Whoa," she said, ducking under his arm and frantically trying to get the key to go into the suddenly impossible-to-find lock.

Michael stilled her trembling hand, took the key, and had the door open in a heartbeat, no small feat considering exactly how fast her heart was pounding.

He rubbed his thumb across her bottom lip. "I gather that's my cue to leave."

Molly summoned up the last remnants of her common sense. "Yes," she agreed.

A man of less conscience would have heard *maybe* in her breathless voice. Michael merely winked. "Soon, sweetheart. Soon."

Molly watched him stroll down the corridor. As soon as the elevator doors closed behind him, she collapsed against the wall. If she'd had a hankie, she'd have waved it to cool her overheated flesh. If she'd lived at Tara a century or so ago, she'd simply have swooned and been done with it. She would have blamed it on her corset, though. Self-deception had its merits, especially when she didn't care to deal with the alternative emotions.

The door across the hall inched open. Liza poked her head out. "Coast clear?"

Molly nodded.

Liza stepped into the hall. "Lordy, lordy," she murmured. "I do believe I felt the earth move clear in there."

"You were watching?" Molly said indignantly. "Everything?"

"Your ex and I had just finished having a depressing tête-à-tête when you arrived. Considering his lousy mood, I couldn't very well abandon you."

Molly grinned. "I don't suppose you ever considered actually announcing your nearby presence or maybe even joining us out here for the festivities?"

"Actually, I saw my role as backup. Not that you needed it with the hunk prepared to rush to your rescue."

"Weren't you satisfied then that I was in good hands?"

"Absolutely."

"And?"

"You wouldn't have wanted me to miss the end, would you? This was definitely R-rated stuff. Maybe X-rated. To be perfectly honest, I was ready to come out here and invite the man in myself if you turned him down."

"I'm glad you controlled yourself."

"Yes, well, with murder uppermost on everyone's mind these days, I figured it was best not to risk it."

"Good thinking."

"Did you-all figure out the killer over quiche?"

"Afraid not. Speaking of which, I'd better get inside and work up a new statement for the media."

Liza shook her head. "I doubt you're going to need one. Vince is on the air as we speak telling the world that he will personally see that the killer of the great Greg Kinsey is brought to justice."

Molly gaped at her. "How does he intend to do that?"

"Beats me. I think it came as a surprise to that Sergeant Jenkins, too. He looked as if he wanted to stuff his beefy hand straight down your boss's throat and rip out his tongue."

"I know the feeling," Molly told her. "It comes over me at least once a day."

Inside her apartment, the phone was ringing. With Liza trailing along behind, she went inside and snatched it up before the answering machine could kick in.

"Molly, it's Veronica Weston. I'm terribly sorry to bother you on your day off, dear, but I have a bit of a problem. You did say you wouldn't mind helping me."

"Of course, Veronica. What can I do?"

"Actually, it's Jeffrey." She lowered her voice to a discreet whisper. "Something's not quite right about this visit. If I didn't know better, I'd say he knows something about the murder."

Molly's breath caught. "You think he did it?"

"Oh, no, of course not," Veronica said in an unconvincing rush. "I just think he knows something he's not telling me."

"Have you asked him if he's keeping something from you?"

"Well, of course I've asked. He simply looks at me with this odd little look in his eyes, then he goes off somewhere. I'm telling you it's giving me the shivers."

"I can understand why that might be disconcerting, but what can I do to help?"

"I thought perhaps we could meet for drinks. You could ask a few pointed questions."

"I think we probably should leave the pointed questions to the police," Molly said nobly. Liza silently applauded, though her expression was disbelieving. Molly scowled at her.

"Besides, if he won't talk to you, why on earth would he talk to me?" she added.

"Actually, since you were here when he arrived and you were with those two policemen, I may have given him the idea that you were here in an official capacity as well."

"You told the man I was a cop!"

"Not specifically," Veronica said offhandedly. "I just sort of left him with that impression. It's not the same thing as lying. You can see that, can't you?"

Actually, Molly thought the distinction was pretty slim. Michael would absolutely love to hear that she was running around town impersonating a police officer. Then, again, perhaps she owed it to Greg to do whatever she could to find out what had happened to him and why. She was only going over to have drinks with the man. What was so terrible about that? The answer to that probably depended a great deal on whom you asked. She decided not to ask anyone.

"I'll be there in half an hour as soon as I make arrangements for my son. Your suite?"

"No, dear. We'll meet you in the lounge in the lobby."

If she hadn't been so busy trying to squash her own guilt, Molly just might have paid more attention to the note of satisfaction in Veronica's silken voice.

• • •

Jeffrey Meyerson looked like a character from a Noel Coward drawing room comedy. Elegant and precise, with a dapper red silk hankerchief tucked in the breast pocket of his white linen jacket, he was armed for his interrogation with a martini in one hand and his rapier wit. Molly might have been charmed if she hadn't been so certain it was all an act.

Veronica sat stiffly by his side, her eyes hidden by her trademark rhinestone-trimmed sunglasses, her brow furrowed with concern. If she'd been aware of the lines the worry sketched on her face, she would have been horrified. She gulped down a double vodka and waved the empty glass imperiously in the direction of the waiter.

"Veronica, dear," Jeffrey scolded mildly. "One's your limit."

She ignored him and reached for the second drink the instant the waiter set it on the table.

"Mr. Meyerson," Molly began.

"Jeffrey."

"Jeffrey, then." She smiled at him. "I'm a little confused about your sudden arrival yesterday. Veronica never mentioned that she was expecting you."

"I told you, my dear, it was to be a surprise. I

simply couldn't bear being away from her another minute. Since I had this trip to Rome, I impulsively decided to route myself through Miami.''

"From Los Angeles?''

His expression grew puzzled. "Of course.''

"Then I must admit, I'm more confused than ever. It was well after midnight when you arrived at the hotel. The last flight from L.A. arrived in Miami hours before that on Saturday.''

"I went by the location before coming to the hotel,'' he said without missing a beat. "That's how I knew about what had happened to Greg. The news was being discussed by everyone. There were policemen all over the place at Veronica's trailer. Naturally, I wanted to learn all I could before coming to the hotel. I knew she would want to hear the latest news.''

"You never once considered that she might be a suspect herself? He was found in her trailer, after all.''

He regarded her indignantly. "Absolutely not. Veronica is not capable of murder. Besides, what reason would she have? Gregory Kinsey idolized her.''

Veronica and Molly both gaped at that, though the actress recovered more quickly than Molly.

"That's a very strong word,'' Molly suggested.

"Strong, but accurate. Everyone knew how badly he wanted her for this film.''

"Did you know Greg yourself?''

"No. I'm sorry to say I never met him.''

"Then you have no idea why he fought so hard on Veronica's behalf?''

Molly watched him closely and caught the faint uneasiness that passed over his face before he shook his head. "No," he said quietly. "I have no idea at all."

The denial was firm, but there wasn't a doubt in Molly's mind that it was also a lie. Veronica was right. There was some secret her fiancé was keeping, and it almost definitely had something to do with the murder.

Her promise to Michael to pass along her theories before she acted on them crossed her mind. She would keep the promise . . . as soon as she knew just a little bit more about what made Jeffrey Meyerson tick.

CHAPTER
EIGHT

Even though she was exhausted, even though she'd promised Brian that she'd spend some time helping him with his summer school science project from hell, even though Michael was likely to be furious, Molly found she couldn't resist temptation. The exit for Southwest Seventh Street was right on her way home. One-way heading west, the street ran parallel to Calle Ocho—Southwest Eighth Street, in the heart of Miami's Little Havana neighborhood.

She drove west as far as Le Jeune, then circled around to come east on Calle Ocho. She passed a park where old men sat playing dominoes. Occasionally the games erupted into violent arguments, but today, in the hot, late afternoon sun, it looked peaceful enough.

Store signs in this section of town were no longer in English. Along with cafés with walk-up windows selling *café cubano* and made-in-the-USA

Havana cigars, *bodegas,* restaurants, *farmacias,* and stores selling statues of the saints, there were also several discreet motels where Latin men took their mistresses for afternoons or evenings of lovemaking.

Hidden behind a line of palm trees, Molly spotted the one where the Italian model and her quick-thinking photographer had reportedly fled the night before. She pulled into the parking lot of the one-story, pale blue stucco motel. Almost all of the spaces were empty. Apparently most of the men who frequented motels such as this did so during the week. Sundays were, no doubt, reserved for families and the sanctity of marriage. Amen.

As she contemplated her next step, second thoughts began sprouting like weeds. She couldn't very well start banging on doors. Nor was she thrilled about walking into the lobby and demanding to see the guest register. She doubted one existed anyway. Her only hope was to find a greedy desk clerk and hand over sufficient cash to loosen his tongue. It all seemed a little tawdry and melodramatic, but she was too curious about the model to back out now.

She clutched twenty bucks and one of her business cards and marched into the tiny reception area, noting that the tiled floor had been swept clean and the furniture polished to a gleam. A bored, overweight clerk glanced up from his racing form, took one look at her, and hurriedly dropped the paper. His smirk was the dirtiest thing in the place.

"English?" Molly inquired hopefully.

"*Sí,*" he said, still leering. "You need room? One hour? All evening?"

Molly laid the twenty-dollar bill on the counter. "I need information."

He regarded the money with interest at first, then with great sorrow. He shook his head. "Sorry, senora. No information."

She hadn't really expected him to be forthcoming. After all, the people who frequented this place expected total anonymity. A clerk who blabbed about the clientele wouldn't last long. At the same time, the Italian was hardly likely to be a regular customer and this man was equally likely to know that.

She placed her business card with its county logo where he could see it. Her thumb just happened to cover the name of her department, leaving her level of official authority open to speculation. For the first time, he began to look uneasy.

"I'm looking for a man, a photographer. He'd have lots of camera equipment with him. Also a beautiful model. Italian. They came here last night, very late."

He listened intently, but she couldn't tell from the blank expression in his eyes if what she was saying didn't register or if such a couple simply hadn't checked in. He glanced around warily, then put his hand over the twenty.

"I not tell you this, *sí*?" he said urgently.

"*Sí,*" Molly agreed.

"*Numero ocho.*"

"They are still there?" she said, and realized she was startled that Officer Jenkins hadn't been here and scared them away.

"*Sí, sí.*" He hurriedly nabbed the money and

shoved it into his pocket. He glanced at his racing form and reached for the phone.

"Gracias," Molly said to his T-shirt-clad back.

Outside she had the creepy feeling that the clerk's lecherous eyes were still on her as she walked along the side of the motel hidden away from the street. A bed of bright red geraniums ran along the wall, the last blossoms wilting in the summer sun. Number eight was at the end, its door freshly painted in pristine white. The drapes were drawn tightly.

Taking a deep breath, Molly knocked hurriedly before she could lose her nerve. She could hear the faint sounds of people scurrying around inside, then sensed someone's gaze on her through the peephole. She knocked again.

She could hear the hushed sounds of what could have been an argument, then the door opened a crack. The face that peered out at her had the calm tranquillity of a Madonna. Only the eyes, dark brown and round as saucers, gave away any hint of fear.

Molly poked her card through the opening in the doorway. The door closed while the chain was removed, then opened again.

Greg's model, if that was indeed who she was, was wearing a skimpy bandeau top and shorts, a revealing outfit Molly wouldn't have dared ten years and ten pounds ago. Thick black hair fell in exotic waves to her shoulders. Her face, with its angles, full pouting lips, and soulful eyes, was a photographer's dream and any man's fantasy. There was an earthy sensuality about the model that was all the more astonishing because she couldn't have been much older than seventeen or eighteen.

Molly glanced into the dimly lit interior beyond her and recognized the photographer she'd met the night before—Giovanni if the taxi dispatcher had gotten it right. He was angrily puffing on a cigarette held between thumb and forefinger in European fashion. He didn't seem pleased by her ingenuity in finding them.

"Why have you come?" he demanded over the sound of Spanish announcers describing a soccer match on TV.

"To speak with your model," Molly said.

"She speaks little English."

Molly didn't take his word for it. She turned to the girl and smiled. She received a tentative smile in return. "You speak English?" Molly asked.

"Yes, I speak some," she said.

"What's your name?"

"Francesca."

"You knew Greg Kinsey?"

Tears shimmered in the girl's eyes. Her words spilled out in a torrent of English and Italian, all mixed together in a way that was beyond Molly's comprehension. The tears tracked down her lovely face and splashed onto her bare shoulders. The photographer lifted his hands in a gesture of helplessness and glared at Molly as if the girl's distress were all her fault.

She led the girl to the bed, murmuring soothingly until she began to calm down.

"Tell me why you and Greg argued," she urged.

Huge brown eyes, still filled with tears, stared back at her in obvious confusion.

"Argued," Molly repeated. "Why did you fight?"

"I'll tell you why they fought," the photographer snapped, taking impatient strides across the room. "He was no good. He made promises."

"What sort of promises?"

He shrugged. "A role in his picture, fame. Who can say what it would take to turn a young girl's head? He made good on none of these promises."

Molly began to see why her pretense of having work for Francesca at the hotel the previous night had met with such disdain. "They fought about this last night?"

The photographer began another tirade, only to be interrupted by Francesca. "No," she said softly. "It was not that way."

Molly held the girl's trembling, ice cold hands. "What way was it then? You tell me."

"I loved him. I wished to stay with him. Here, in Miami. He told me to go home."

The photographer suddenly looked defeated. "He was a fool," he murmured in a way that told Molly that he himself was enchanted by this child-woman. Had he been furious that the director had rejected her? Or that he had dared to take her as his lover in the first place? Had he been angry enough to kill Greg?

"Were you there when they argued?" Molly inquired.

"No," he said at once. "I came after . . ."

"After what?" she said.

"After they argued," he said swiftly. Too swiftly?

As if he'd guessed her thoughts, he said, "He was alive when we left."

Francesca was nodding as well. "He was alive." Her voice broke as she added softly, "It was the last time I saw him so."

"And you left together?"

The photographer glanced at Francesca as if trying to communicate with her silently. To Molly he said simply, "We left together."

Molly gazed into Francesca's troubled eyes and knew that the photographer was lying. But why? Was he protecting the woman he loved with the fabricated alibi? Or himself?

It was beginning to seem that there must have been a steady stream of people in and out of that trailer, all in a scant matter of minutes—Veronica, Francesca, Giovanni, and, if those three were to be believed, the killer.

Although she didn't entirely dismiss the girl and the photographer as suspects, she asked, "Did you see anyone else near the trailer?"

Francesca shook her head. "No one."

"The policemen was at the end of the block," Giovanni said. "Otherwise, no one."

Molly recalled where the off-duty officers had been stationed to keep out curiosity seekers. The side street where Veronica's trailer had been was cordoned off at both ends of the block with guards at each end. Others stood guard along the stretch of Ocean Drive where the actual filming was taking place in front of a Deco hotel.

"How did you get past the policemen in the first place?" she asked.

"Gregory had introduced me to them," Francesca said. "He had given me a pass." She reached into her huge purse and rummaged around, finally extracting a slip of bright yellow paper. "You see? It gave me permission to enter."

GK Productions had issued permanent passes to all those connected with the film. Guests of the cast and crew were given similar slips with specific dates filled in and initialed by Laura Crain. No one was allowed on location without one of those slips.

Molly studied Francesca's slip and noted that it had been signed by Greg himself, not Laura, and that it was open-ended. It was unlikely that either of the guards would have argued with the director's authority, despite whatever instructions Laura had given them.

"You have one of these as well?" she asked Giovanni.

He shook his head. "I came onto the street through an alley. They did not see me."

Which meant that anyone could have done the same, Molly deduced. So much for the sanctity of the set. The list of suspects did not have to be limited to those connected with the film, after all. Anyone determined enough and familiar with that alley access could have slipped onto the street and away again without ever being seen by one of the guards.

Molly sighed. Instead of filling in gaps of what she knew, it seemed she was only raising more questions.

"Thank you for seeing me," she told them. "Will you stay on here?"

"The police have told us to stay, yes," Giovanni said. "We wish to cooperate. I did not like this man Gregory Kinsey, but I have respect for his work. I did not wish to see him die."

"Then the police know you are here?"

"They know, yes."

"Will you stay here or move back to Miami Beach?"

"Here is best. There are no memories for her. Hopefully it won't be for long."

Molly noticed that Francesca was twisting a rosary in her hands. If the strand of beads was wound much tighter, it would snap. Francesca's eyes were filled with sadness, and suddenly Molly realized that she was perhaps the only one who truly mourned Greg Kinsey.

She placed her hand over the girl's. "If you would like to talk, call me," she said impulsively. "I'll leave my card on the dresser."

Francesca bit her lower lip to stop the trembling. She nodded. Giovanni stepped closer and laid a hand on her shoulder. He murmured something in Italian that drew her gaze up to meet his. She smiled tremulously.

"That is better, *cara mia*," he said. He glanced at Molly as she went to the door. "Francesca will be fine. I will see to that."

Feeling more exhausted than ever, Molly quietly shut the door and walked to her car. As she pulled out of the lot and headed east on Eighth Street, she caught a glimpse of the driver of a car just turning into the motel. Unless she was very much mistaken, the driver was Otis Jenkins. She doubted the detective was there to rent a room. If Francesca and Giovanni blabbed about her visit, she was going to be in even deeper hot water with the Miami Beach Police Department.

So what else was new? She didn't regret tracking down the model and the photographer one bit. It gave her more pieces of the puzzle to use when she tried to explain things to Vince in the morning. Unfortunately, the only piece of information her boss was likely to be interested in was the name of the killer, and she was no closer to knowing that than she had been before.

At home Brian and Liza were in the dining room with some sort of contraption rigged up on the dining room table. Water was everywhere. Molly eyed the mess warily. "What is it?"

"A desal . . . a desal something," Brian said, regarding it proudly. "Pretty awesome, huh, Mom?"

"A desalinization device," Liza corrected. "It's a winner, if I do say so myself."

"It's awesome," Molly agreed, trying to sound enthusiastic, rather than thunderstruck. "I don't suppose either of you considered putting some plastic under it, so the water wouldn't destroy the finish on the dining room table."

Liza and Brian glanced guiltily at the spotted surface. "Think of it this way," Liza said. "He'll probably be able to sell this thing to the government and make a fortune. You can buy a new table."

"Is it finished?" she inquired cautiously.

"Yeah. It's great. Want to see it work?" Brian asked.

She sat down. "Go to it," she said more enthusiastically. If sacrificing the dining room table meant her son never had to know how little she understood science, it was a small price to pay. Last year's project, which had gotten a paltry C-minus, had nearly robbed her of her sanity. This one looked like an A to her.

Later, with the science project safely in its box and Brian tucked into bed, she fell gratefully into her own bed. But instead of getting some much needed sleep, she spent another restless night pondering the intricate web of lies being spun around Greg Kinsey's death.

Love—or some of its darker permutations—had made suspects of a wide variety of people connected with the director. Even though she was convinced if they could unravel the lies they would identify the killer, she had no idea which thread to tug on first.

CHAPTER
NINE

Sitting in the Metro/Dade film office in the old Vizcaya estate gatehouse with Molly and Jeannette, Vince waved a handful of newspaper clippings in their faces on Monday morning. It was the first time Vince had been in the office before nine in all the years Molly had worked for him.

Vince explained to anyone who asked that he had to stay later in the evening for all of the office's West Coast contacts. Those who didn't ask already knew that he tried to fit at least nine holes of golf into the early morning hours. When nothing was on his calendar, he went ahead and played the full eighteen. It took a crisis of major proportions for him to schedule anything before noon. Molly supposed the murder qualified.

As the clippings fluttered, Molly managed to catch mastheads from half the major papers in the

U.S., plus a couple from overseas. The headlines in English were not encouraging.

"It's a disaster," he said, confirming her own quick analysis. His expression was accusing. "How could you let this happen? The reason I sent you over there to baby-sit this production was to keep everybody happy. I assumed you knew that also meant they should stay alive."

Jeannette shot Molly a sympathetic look as Vince's tirade went on. "I've had calls from the county manager, half a dozen different local mayors, to say nothing of tourism officials and the film liaison in Orlando who can't wait to snatch victory out of the jaws of our defeat," he said. "Are you trying to destroy this office?"

"Excuse me?" Molly said incredulously.

Jeannette muttered under her breath in Creole. Molly had a feeling that if she'd known exactly what the Haitian clerk was saying, she would have echoed it. Their boss had a way of viewing all calamities in relation to the safety of his own neck.

"I did not kill Gregory Kinsey," Molly reminded him slowly and emphatically. "I could hardly cover up the man's death. Did you want me to dump the body in the Everglades and hope that nobody noticed the man was missing? Maybe I should have finished directing the picture myself."

Vince gaped at her sarcasm. Finally his shoulders sagged, and he dropped the clippings on his cluttered desk. "No, of course not. How are we going to handle this, though? Do you realize that I had half a dozen calls at home over the weekend from producers we've been trying to lure to south Florida? They're all very nervous."

"I think you can safely reassure them that we do not have a serial killer on the loose who's targeting Hollywood directors," Molly said dryly.

"You don't know that."

Molly rolled her gaze heavenward and prayed for patience. "Okay, Vince, what would you like me to do?"

"We have to solve this thing as quickly as possible if we're going to minimize the damage. Talk to that cop friend of yours, the one who worked on the murder in your building."

"I have talked to him. It's not in his jurisdiction. He's with Metro, not Miami Beach."

"But he's good, right?"

"He's good."

"Then I'll take care of it."

Molly didn't like the sound of that. She had a strong hunch Michael would like it even less. "What are you going to do?" she asked cautiously.

"Don't give it another thought," Vince said, looking more cheerful. "Just get the hell over to GK Productions and do whatever you can to keep them from packing up and fleeing to L.A. to finish this in the studio. Take Jeannette with you," he added magnanimously. "She can answer phones, take dictation, whatever they need."

Molly cast a look at the thirty-year-old Haitian woman with the close-cropped hair and regal bearing. She was the bane of Vince's existence. Her round mahogany face was totally devoid of expression, but Molly could detect the twinkle in her eyes.

Jeannette loved to mutter darkly in Creole whenever Vince irritated her. He was convinced she was putting a curse on him. Because she was damn good at her job, he couldn't fire her, but he grabbed at any opportunity to send her on whatever assignments he could justify out of the office.

Molly hid a grin. Vince and Jeannette must have really been going at it this morning, if he was ready to loan her out to a production company. Since Molly was anxious to get to GK Productions herself, she didn't waste time arguing that the county might look askance at paying a clerk's salary so she could answer someone else's phones.

"Come on, Jeannette, let's get going. I'm sure they'll be thrilled with the extra help."

GK Productions had taken up an entire floor of one of the most recently renovated Ocean Drive deco hotels. Since it was off-season for Miami Beach, Molly had been able to help them get fantastic rates for the offices and for the cast's housing. They'd even redecorated their best suite for Veronica.

Laura Crain, Hank Murdock, and production assistant Jerry Shaw were huddled around a table in Crain's third-floor hotel suite when Molly and Jeannette arrived just after nine thirty. She'd hoped for a few minutes alone with the normally late rising producer, but obviously the current production crisis had changed everyone's sleep schedule.

Or possibly, Molly thought, judging from the overall appearance of exhaustion, the trio had been up all night. An ashtray overflowed with cigarette butts and a room service cart was littered with the remains of some unidentifiable meal. Dinner? Midnight snack? Breakfast? It was impossible to tell from the congealed leftovers. Jerry was clutching the receivers of two phones, speaking alternately into each of them. He looked desperate.

She introduced Jeannette to everyone and explained that Vince had sent her along to help out in any way they needed her to. Laura Crain started to say something, but Hank stopped her with a look.

"Great," he said. "These phones have been ringing off the hook. Jerry can't keep up with the calls. Another hour of this and he'll be back in his room having a nervous breakdown."

"Just tell me what you'd like me to say," Jeannette said, "and I'll get to work."

While Hank gave her instructions and Jerry gratefully relinquished the phones, Molly asked for a cup of coffee. "Is there any left?" she said, moving automatically toward the room service serving cart.

"I've just ordered up another pot," Laura said. "Should be here any minute."

"It looks as if you all have been at this for a while," Molly observed.

"Since last night," Hank said. "I'm getting too damned old to miss this many hours of sleep."

"We had to make some decisions," Laura retorted sharply. She looked every bit as brittle as she sounded. Her makeup had long since worn off, leaving her pale. Her green eyes glittered too brightly. Her hair was mussed and she twisted one strand around a finger. Molly doubted it would take much for her to snap. Oddly, though, today there was little obvious evidence of grief for a just-murdered lover.

"Every day we're shut down costs us thousands," Laura said. "We were already over budget. I spent all day yesterday on the phone with the head of the studio trying to convince him not to scrap the project and eat the losses. Fortunately, half of his key executives were away from L.A. for the weekend, so they couldn't get together and compare notes until today. When they call here around noon, we'd better have a plan or we'll be on the next plane home with an unfinished picture that will never see the light of day."

Molly already knew how Vince would take that news. She'd be lucky if he didn't fire her. Come to think of it, they'd all be lucky if Dade County didn't simply drop the department from its budget. There were already some who considered a film office frivolous. They seemed to think production companies would swarm to Miami whether anyone smoothed the way for them or not.

"What do you expect to happen?" she asked Laura.

"They'll moan and groan and threaten a little. Then they'll agree to giving us another two weeks," she said confidently. "If Hank takes over now and we don't lose another minute of production time, we have a chance of bringing this in close enough to budget to keep everyone reasonably happy."

Molly watched for Hank's reaction. If he was eager to direct the rest of the picture and hoped to negotiate an on-screen credit with Greg for bailing them out, he hid it well. If anything, he looked resigned rather than elated.

Even so, Molly had a hard time imagining anyone's not being thrilled at the amount of attention this picture was likely to generate, no matter how the reviews turned out. The simple fact that it was Greg Kinsey's last picture would draw curiosity seekers to the theaters in droves.

"This could be quite a break for you, couldn't it?" she said to Hank.

Rather than reacting with outrage or deliberate innocence, Hank regarded her with amusement. "Playing detective, Molly?"

She felt heat steal into her cheeks. "You have to admit that taking over as director on a Greg Kinsey film could be construed as a motive for murder."

"It could," he said agreeably. "But I was in the production trailer with half a dozen other people at the time Greg was murdered. You found me there yourself."

Molly tried to recall the scene in that trailer when she'd gone in search of Greg. Hank had been seated at the table, a cup of coffee in hand. Jerry and several others had been playing poker at that same table, but there had been no cards in front of Hank. Because he'd just returned from murdering Greg?

"Why weren't you in on the poker game?" she asked.

"I don't gamble. Haven't in years. Lost too much of my pay at the tables in Vegas."

"Why are we wasting time discussing this?" Laura demanded. "The cops have questioned all of us. We don't need to be answering her questions as well."

"I'm just trying to help," Molly countered.

"How? By pointing a finger at one of us to get some local psycho off the hook?"

"Where were you?" Molly retorted before she could stop herself. "You weren't in the production trailer."

Molly wouldn't have been surprised if Laura ignored the blunt question, but the producer actually seemed anxious to share her alibi.

"No, I wasn't in the trailer," she said. "I was back here taking care of business. That's what Greg hired me to do. He hated the paperwork, hated dealing with all the numbers guys at the studio."

Molly knew that was true enough. Laura did have the organizational and logistical skills of an army general. She'd moved the cast and crew around town with a minimum of fuss. She could identify every one of the locals hired, practically right down to their Social Security numbers. Unfortunately, she didn't waste a lot of time on charm. Other than Greg, and possibly Hank, Molly wasn't sure anyone got along with her.

Before she could ask Laura if anyone had actually seen her at the hotel at the time of the murder, an argument broke out in the adjoining room. The connecting door burst open and Daniel Ortiz stormed in.

A Dodgers baseball cap covered his prematurely graying dark hair. A religious medallion dangled from a chain around his neck, providing an interesting contrast to the bloodred logo of some heavy metal rock group that adorned his black T-shirt. He was trailed by two men Molly recognized as key technical experts on *Endless Tomorrows*. As she recalled, one had something to do with sound, the other with lighting.

"We've got a problem," Ortiz told Laura, dropping a handful of pages on the table in front of her. "There's no way to do all these scenes in the same day. No way. What the hell were you thinking of?"

"I was thinking of trying to make up some of the time we lost. Hank said we could do it."

Ortiz did not spare the new director a glance. He kept his attention on Laura. "I do not do schlock. If we push like this, there will be mistakes. Paul and Ken agree."

"Do Paul and Ken also agree they'd rather shut down production now?" Laura inquired.

The director of photography finally looked at Hank. "Is that the choice?"

Hank nodded, looking fairly miserable. "I hate it, too, but Laura's right. We're going to have to make some compromises. Work with me on this and maybe we can pull it off."

The director of photography took off his cap and shoved his hand through his thick hair. He stared out the window for several minutes, then nodded abruptly. "If this is what we have to do, then it's what we'll do. Come on, Hank. Let's see what we can figure out."

When Hank had left the room with the others, Molly sat down next to Laura. "Daniel owns part of GK Productions, doesn't he?"

Laura regarded her warily. "Still playing amateur sleuth, Molly? It's a dangerous game," she warned.

"Come on," Molly pleaded. "Help me out

here. You must want to see Greg's killer caught as much as anyone.''

After a momentary hesitation, her gaze challenging, Laura finally rubbed her eyes with the back of her hand and sighed.

"Okay, yes," she said. "Of course, I want to see Greg's killer caught, but I can't start thinking about all that now. If I do, I'll come unglued. Greg placed a lot of faith in me when he gave me this job. I can't let him down.''

"He was your mentor?''

"Yes.''

"How does Daniel Ortiz fit in?''

"He and Greg went to film school together. They did their student project together. It was a natural fit. He may not have liked it, but Greg knew how to talk with the money guys, how to get the most out of an actor. Daniel knows how to capture it on film.''

"What happens to GK Productions with Greg dead?''

Laura shook her head. "I don't know. The company's not worth much with Greg gone, unless Hank can prove himself on this picture. Frankly, he's a decent director, maybe even better than Greg, but he's too low-key, too content to be second-in-command. It takes ambition to make it in this business, and Hank's not driven enough to really scramble for the top spot. It was a good match. He bailed Greg out whenever Greg started drinking or womanizing. He did it too damned much. Greg never had to grow up.''

The last was said with an edge of bitterness.

Molly recognized that it was as close as Laura was likely to come to an admission that she recognized Greg's flaws and hated him for them.

"Are you so sure Hank wasn't tired of bailing Greg out? Maybe he'd had to do it one time too many," Molly suggested.

Laura's eyes glinted angrily. "No, dammit. Hank did not kill Greg. For all I know you did it yourself. You had the hots for him. I saw that the first day you showed up on the set. You were hanging around all the time, ready to do any little thing he asked of you."

"Usurping your role," Molly shot back. "Were you jealous, Laura? Maybe not of me, but how about the model Greg discovered a few days ago? Did his affair with her make you furious enough to kill him?"

Laura looked as if Molly had pierced her heart with a knife. "What Greg and I had was special, damn you. Don't try to take that away from me. Don't," she said softly, brushing fiercely at the tears that ran down her cheeks.

Before Molly could apologize, Laura jumped up and ran into the bathroom, locking the door behind her. Molly heard the water start to run and looked helplessly at Jeannette, who shook her head as she listened to someone at the other end of the phone line. She held the phone out. "It's for you."

Molly was still trying to figure out if Laura's outburst stemmed from despair or guilt. She reluctantly walked over to take the phone. "Who is it?" she asked Jeannette.

"He didn't give his name. His tone didn't encourage questions."

"Molly DeWitt."

"Mrs. DeWitt, this is Sergeant Jenkins. I want you at the Miami Beach Police Station."

"When?"

"Now," he said tersely and slammed the phone down.

Molly didn't have any trouble guessing what the detective wanted. No doubt he had a few questions about her presence at the motel the previous afternoon.

CHAPTER
TEN

The area around the Miami Beach Police Department on Washington Avenue was in a state of evolution. Two blocks west of Ocean Drive, Washington was a hybrid of old-style open-air fruit markets, trendy restaurants, discount pharmacies, and souvenir shops. Nightclubs appealing to the young bumped right into shops supplying wheelchairs and canes for the elderly. Garish china flamingos and gaudy T-shirts were sold next to yuppie fashions. The old Fifth Street Gym, where top boxers had trained for decades, was only a few blocks away. Parking was at a premium.

Molly found a metered spot two blocks over and made her way to the fancy new police headquarters. The made-over building was at least three or four times the size of the cramped old structure that had been an easy stroll from the famed Joe's, where chilled stone crabs had become a world-class delicacy.

Molly walked into the brightly lit police station lobby and immediately felt like a criminal. No doubt, after the meddling she'd done the previous day, she deserved to.

Reporter Ted Ryan, his shirttail pulled loose, his tie askew, came rushing down the hall after her. "Molly, wait. I really need to talk to you."

"Not now." She wanted to get her meeting with Jenkins and its likely lecture over with. With production scheduled to begin again in the morning, she had plenty to do to help smooth the way.

"At least tell me what you're doing here," Ted pleaded. "Has there been a break in the case?"

Molly stopped reluctantly and shook her head. "Not that I'm aware of."

"Then what? You didn't come all the way over here just to chat."

"Maybe I did," she replied. "Some of my best friends are policemen."

Ted looked desperate. "Come on, Molly. How about we trade information?"

Molly studied him thoughtfully. It wouldn't hurt to know what the word on the street was about the murder. Ted would have heard all the latest rumors by now. "What information do you have?"

He shook his head. "You first."

"Oh, no. You want anything out of me, you cough up what you have first. I can always wait to read it in the morning paper."

Reluctantly, Ted opened his notebook and flipped through a few pages. "Okay, here it is. According to my sources, they've assigned someone new to take over the case. My guess is it's that hot-shot friend of yours, Michael O'Hara.''

"Oh, my God," Molly murmured under her breath. She saw a bench up ahead and sank onto it. Ted sat beside her. She looked him straight in the eye. "Are you sure?"

Ted nodded. "The guy who told me is pretty reliable. O'Hara was on the scene the other night. It all hangs together."

"But he's Metro. And he just happened to drop by Saturday night. He wasn't working. I can swear to that." As she caught Ted scribbing, she added, "Off the record, of course."

"Molly!"

"You want to cost me my job? All I can say on the record is that the Metro/Dade film office deeply regrets the death of Gregory Kinsey, while on location here. Period. End of statement."

Ted rolled his eyes in disgust.

"I know, but that's all I'm allowed to say for attribution," she said. "Anything else I say is just background. You'll have to get it officially from someone else. Now why do you think a Metro cop has been assigned to take over the case?"

"The way I hear it someone demanded he be brought in to try and solve this thing before the publicity gets out of hand." He regarded her slyly. "You wouldn't know anything about that, would you?"

"No," Molly said weakly. She tried to inject a note of conviction into her voice. "No. Absolutely not."

Ted grinned. "Methinks . . ."

"Don't think, Ted. Isn't that one of the first tenets of sound journalism? Stick strictly to the facts. No suppositions. No guesswork. No thinking."

"Then it's true," he gloated. "I knew it."

Before he could take any more wild leaps of logic and wind up with confirmation of some other theory he'd developed over the past forty-eight hours, Molly raced down the hall. She had no idea exactly where Sergeant Jenkins's office was, but from the argument that was echoing off the walls she had a pretty good idea. At least one of the voices sounded all too familiar. So did the tone.

Molly skidded to a halt and looked through a window into a cramped office that looked as if a hurricane had recently passed through. She stopped just in time to see the Miami Beach detective slam his phone back into the cradle. He glowered at Michael, who was fiddling with a pair of sunglasses. Michael jammed the glasses back on his face and scowled, then took them off again.

"Well?" he said.

"Dammit, you know what the chief said," Jenkins retorted. "He confirmed it. You're on the Kinsey case. Of all the jackass moves, you son of a bitch. Don't you have enough to worry about on your own turf?"

"Dammit, Jenkins, I don't like this any better than you do, but we're stuck with it. Let's try to make it work."

"Hell, no," Jenkins said with exaggerated generosity. "You want the case this bad, it's yours."

"I do not want the case," Michael retorted, biting off each word.

"Yeah, sure. I'm supposed to believe that."

"It's the truth."

Molly felt as if she were trying to watch a tennis match from the vantage point of the net. Sergeant Jenkins served up another sly dig about Michael walking off in the middle of his own investigation.

"Couldn't break that case, so now you're over here messing in mine."

"I'm here because somebody in the county wants it that way. I'm beginning to see why," Michael shot back, jamming his sunglasses into place.

That was a sure sign that he was losing his temper. Molly had observed that he used those sunglasses to shut out the world when he'd lost patience with it nearly as often as he did to shade his eyes.

Sergeant Jenkins still wasn't content to let it rest. "I can see the press hasn't labeled you an ambitious hotshot for nothing. With an ego that size, I'm surprised you bother with us lowly mortals at all," he said, and stalked from the office.

He was so angry he didn't even notice Molly as he stormed by. Just her luck. Considering the furious expression on Michael's face, she might have been better off with Jenkins.

When Michael finally glanced Molly's way, she stepped into the office and inquired innocently, "All done being territorial?"

Michael lifted his hands in the air in a gesture of total frustration. "The man's a jerk. I didn't ask to be assigned to this case. The way I've got it figured, your boss whined to my boss, who whined to the

County Commission, and the next thing I know I'm meddling in a case that belongs to the Miami Beach Police Department.''

He came over until they were toe to toe. She forced herself not to retreat. He removed his glasses so Molly could get a glimpse of his cold, hard stare. "Now how do you suppose that happened?''

Molly winced. "You sound as if you're blaming me.''

"If the shoe fits.''

"It doesn't. Vince whined, not me.''

"But who put the notion into his head? You're not suggesting that someone just drew my name out of a hat, are you?''

Molly tried to recall her exact conversation with her boss. Unfortunately there might have been the tiniest hint that Michael O'Hara could get to the bottom of Gregory's murder and end this public relations nightmare for the film office. Whether it was Vince's conclusion or hers hardly seemed to matter. Michael was here and she had a pretty good idea why.

"No,'' she said meekly. "I might have mentioned your name when Vince asked who solved that murder in my building.''

"I'm delighted the two of you hold me in such high regard, but the next time you get yourself tangled up in a murder, make sure it's in my jurisdiction if you want me to be involved. I don't like butting heads with other cops, especially when they're perfectly competent.''

Hoping to get herself off the hook, Molly reminded him, "You just called Otis Jenkins a jerk.''

"It's his general attitude I'm not crazy about. There's nothing wrong with his intelligence or his credentials. I don't even blame him for being mad as hell. I'm mad as hell. I was in the middle of another case, not as flashy maybe, but the guy was just as dead and his family is justifiably concerned with catching the killer."

Molly winced. "You were pulled off that case?"

"Practically in the middle of an interrogation."

"Someone took over for you, though, right?"

"Sure. Some other overloaded detective got another case dumped in his lap, so I could come over here and baby-sit this investigation."

"I've got a motive worked out for Hank Murdock," Molly said, hoping to distract him.

He responded in terse Spanish. She knew the word for "thank you." The phrase he'd uttered hadn't sounded much like that. Neither had the tone.

"Don't you want to hear it?"

He sat down in Jenkins's chair. "Sure. Why not. Start by telling me again who this Murdock is."

Neither his tone nor his expression was exactly inviting, but she told him anyway. "Assistant director. My impression is that he's always stayed in the background. You know the kind, competent but not ambitious. In fact, that's exactly how Laura Crain described him. Now *Endless Tomorrows* is practically dumped in his lap. A lot of people will be watching to see if he can sustain Greg's level of creativity."

"How old's this guy?"

"Forty-five. Maybe fifty, but I don't think so."

"Let me see if I'm following you here. You think

this guy who is forty-five, maybe fifty, and has never displayed any sign of burning ambition decides to off the director of this particular film so he can finally have his big break? Is that right?"

Molly felt her cheeks burn. "It doesn't sound so logical when you say it."

"It isn't," he said flatly. "Not unless the man is having a mid-life crisis of gargantuan proportions."

She glared at him. "There's no need to be so sarcastic. I'm just trying to help."

The reminder didn't seem to placate him. "What are you doing here anyway?" he inquired. "Shouldn't you be on location holding Veronica Weston's hand or offering assistance to that barracuda who's in charge of production?"

"Sergeant Jenkins summoned me here. I'm not sure exactly why," she said, figuring Michael was in no mood to hear the specifics. Naturally, though, he couldn't leave well enough alone.

He regarded her suspiciously. "Now why would Jenkins want to talk to you?"

"I can't imagine."

"Molly?"

"Really, you'll have to ask him. I guess since he's gone, I might as well take off, too." She backed to the door. "You want a lift over to the location?"

He shook his head. "No, thanks. I'll be going with Jenkins."

"I don't think so."

"Why not?"

"He just pulled out of the parking lot. If anyone else had pulled into traffic the way he just did, the chief himself would have gone out to ticket him."

"Damn," Michael muttered. He was on his feet and across the office before she could blink. He yanked open the door, then glanced back at her. "Well, come on. There's no point in trying to find two parking places on Ocean Drive."

"You're welcome," Molly grumbled.

If he caught the remark, he chose to ignore it. When they reached her convertible, he held out his hand for the keys. "I'll drive."

"Hoping to strand me without a car again?"

"It's a thought."

"You really are in a nasty mood. Don't take it out on me."

He drummed his fingers on the steering wheel as they waited for an old lady pushing a shopping cart filled with groceries to cross the street. From the set of his jaw, she guessed he was struggling between fury over the circumstances in which he'd found himself and his normal decent manners.

"Sorry," he said as if the word were one with which he was slightly unfamiliar.

She nodded. It was nice that she'd been able to wrench an apology out of him. She had a hunch, though, that the tentative peace they'd reached was likely to give way to another round of verbal warfare once she admitted the real reason Jenkins had probably called her to the station. She figured she might as well get the confession out of the way.

"Remember that model? The one Greg was supposedly involved with?"

Michael turned toward her. "Yes," he said very slowly. "What about her?"

Before she could say a word, he apparently read the answer on her face. "You didn't talk to her?"

"Actually, I did," she said in a rush. "The photographer, too."

Michael slammed his hand on the steering wheel. "I don't suppose you just happened to run into them sunning themselves on the beach?"

She shook her head. "I went to the motel. I bribed the desk clerk to tell me which room they were in."

"Are you out of your mind?"

"Do you want to hear this or not?"

"Fine. Of course. Tell me what you discovered on this little adventure."

"Her name's Francesca. She admits she and Greg fought. She was furious because Greg didn't want her to stay behind with him. The photographer was furious because he's in love with her and he resented the way Greg used her and dumped her. They both had motives and opportunity, but they both swear he was alive when they left him in Veronica's trailer Saturday night."

"And you believed them?"

"I believed her. Him, I'm not so sure about."

"Why?"

"I told you, he was jealous. Besides, he all but warned her right in front of me to keep something a secret."

"Like what?"

"He said they left together. Then he looked at Francesca as if he was trying to tell her not to contradict him."

"That's one possibility. The other is that he's protecting her."

"Yeah, I know. What are you going to do next?"

He pulled the car into a tight space at the oceanfront curb, then removed his sunglasses long enough to look her straight in the eye. "I'm surprised you intend to leave the next step up to me."

"You are the detective," she said dutifully.

"Try to remember that."

"By the way, I almost forgot. Jeffrey Meyerson has an excuse for the delay between the arrival of his flight and the time he showed up at Veronica's hotel room. He stopped by the location first."

Michael groaned. "Don't tell me. Let me guess. You've talked to him, too."

"Well, Veronica did call me and ask me to come by," she said defensively. "She was worried that he might know something about the murder."

"And did he?"

"Not that I could discover."

"Any other little tidbits I should know about? Things perhaps the police haven't stumbled on yet?"

Molly smiled brightly. "Nope. None that I can think of."

"I'm sure you'll let me know if you just happen across some evidence."

"Absolutely."

Michael put a hand on her elbow and turned her to face him. "Molly, I'm serious about this. Can I trust you to pass on whatever you discover, however insignificant it may seem to you?"

"Of course you can trust me," she said indignantly.

"Can I?" he said. "You made me the same promise just yesterday."

"And just look at all the information I gave you today."

He shook his head. "There's no arguing with you, is there? You have an answer for everything."

"I try," she said, purposely ignoring his exasperated tone. "You may not believe this, but I really do appreciate the fact that you listen to me. You take what I tell you seriously . . . even when you are furious with me."

For an instant he looked taken aback. Then a faint smile touched his lips and was gone. "Yeah, well, don't ever tell anyone I said this, but you've got good instincts when it comes to people."

"Just think what I could do if I had access to an evidence lab and a few crackerjack technicians," she said, winking at him as she went off to take the elevator back to Laura Crain's suite.

"Don't even think about it," he warned as the doors of the elevator slid shut. They didn't close quite fast enough, though. She still heard the unmistakable sound of his laughter.

CHAPTER
ELEVEN

Molly figured she'd escaped the worst of Michael's wrath. Despite his anger and his protests, she felt much better knowing that he was on the case. In fact, she was downright cheerful as she went back into the production office.

Jeannette looked far more harried than she ever did in the film office, even on the worst days with Vince on her case. She glanced up from the phones and waved Molly over. When she'd put the caller on hold, she asked, "You have anyplace else you can be for the next couple of hours?"

Molly shook her head. "Why?"

"You might want to stay out of Laura Crain's path. She's convinced you carried some tale off to the police that explains why both Daniel and Hank were called in for questioning. They just left in the middle of one of her production meetings and went downstairs."

Molly glanced around the room. Jerry Shaw was the only other person in here, and he was busy scribbling all over one of the scripts. "Where's Laura now?" Molly asked.

"The bathroom." The normally unflappable Jeannette looked genuinely distressed. "You sure you don't have urgent business back at the office? She is a crazy one."

Molly shook her head. "I can't run off and have her accuse me of abandoning her in her hour of need. You can imagine how Vince would love that. I'll stay here and take my chances. Thanks for warning me, though."

She crossed the room and stopped by the production assistant. "Hi, Jerry. Anything I can do to help?"

He looked up at her and shook his head.

Molly persisted. "Has tomorrow's schedule been worked out? I can start coordinating with the Beach authorities as soon as I know what locations you need."

"You'll have to ask Laura. She keeps changing her mind. It's driving everyone crazy."

"Why isn't Hank making the decisions?"

Jerry blinked at her. "Well, he is. Sort of. Laura keeps countermanding him. She's better at logistics and stuff. She wants Jonathan to make some adjustments to the script that'll speed things along. Daniel and Hank agreed, but no one can find him."

"Maybe he got tired of everyone ignoring his suggestions," Molly said.

"Not everyone. Just Veronica. She made the guy's life a living hell. If I were him, I'd be back in

L.A. by now. Laura made sure that wouldn't happen. She's holding all the tickets."

"Has he checked out?"

"No. He's just laying low."

"Then maybe he's on the beach or having lunch at one of the cafés."

"Could be, but I don't have time to go look for him. I have to finish these script notes. Could you try to track him down?"

Since looking for the writer beat waiting for Laura to throw one of her tantrums, Molly agreed.

She found thirty-year-old Jonathan Fine some fifteen minutes later on the porch of a hotel five blocks south. He was sipping what looked like a double shot of Scotch and staring at the ocean, his expression bleak. Molly slid into the seat across from him, wondering how he stood the glare and scorching heat of the direct midsummer sun. She was drenched in perspiration just from walking a few blocks in the humid, 88-degree weather. It probably helped that each time the hotel door opened a rush of cool air breezed past.

"Hi," she said, taking in the rumpled shirt with its exotic and colorful flowers and the khaki shorts. The clothes contrasted sharply with his bookish horn-rimmed glasses. He looked like a writer's idea of what a screenwriter in Florida ought to look like. He also looked as if he'd feel more comfortable in a three-piece suit with his blond hair trimmed to executive neatness, instead of scraping his collar as it was now.

"You looking for me?" he asked, barely sparing her a glance. He sounded as miserable as he looked.

Molly nodded. "Laura wants some changes in the script."

"So what else is new?" he said. If anything, he looked even more woebegone. He turned his gaze on Molly. "Maybe you can explain why they bought it in the first place. About the only thing left from the original is the title, and I understand some marketing guy at the studio hates that."

"It must be frustrating. This is your first feature film, isn't it?"

He nodded. "Yeah. I used to be in a business that made sense."

"What was that?"

"Banking."

No wonder he looked as if he ought to be wearing a suit. "From what I've seen of banks collapsing, you may have gotten out of that just in the nick of time. How did you sell the script to Greg?"

"He banked at my branch in Santa Monica. One day there was a problem with his account and we got to talking. I told him I'd been working on this script. I'm sure people said that to him all the time, but he asked to see it. After he read it, he called me. He actually said then that he liked it."

Jonathan finished off his drink. "Greg helped me find an agent, took out an option, and then started trying to put the financing together. Everybody told me it was a fluke, that I shouldn't quit my day job, but would I listen? No. I was so sure this was it, my ticket to fame and fortune. Jesus, was I naïve."

"What you accomplished is pretty incredible," Molly said. "I've seen the statistics. The odds are against a beginner breaking in with a first script."

"But how am I supposed to reconcile what's on the screen with what I put on paper? Duke likes to ad lib and Greg let him. He said Duke's an instinctive actor."

"You don't agree?"

"It's bull. He just can't memorize his damn lines. As for Veronica, she wants to play the role like she's still twenty-seven. If the script had called for a woman that age, Greg wouldn't have cast her. She blames me for making her seem old."

"What'll happen now that Greg's dead?"

"God knows. Hank can't control the cast and Laura's more interested in the bottom line."

He sighed heavily and blinked several times behind his thick-lensed glasses. "Sorry. You didn't come chasing after me to listen to my gripes. What do you need?"

Molly winced. "Actually, Laura . . ."

"Has a few changes. You said that. I guess I blocked it. Well, come on. I might as well get it over with."

He staggered a little as he stood up, then squared his shoulders. Molly wondered if perhaps she should have insisted on coffee before dragging him back to the hotel.

"Are you working on another script?" she asked.

For the first time he gave her a rueful grin. "Yeah, this one. Maybe once it's done, I'll be able to write something that a director and the stars will actually love as it is. I'm not holding my breath, though."

Molly wondered idly if Jonathan Fine was disturbed enough over what had happened to his script to murder the man responsible. She dismissed the thought immediately. He seemed too mild-mannered to shoot someone in cold blood. If he was anything like other writers she had known, though, he probably had a keen eye for human frailties.

"Tell me something," Molly said. "You know everyone connected with the film. Have you had any thoughts on who might have shot Greg?"

Jonathan stared at her, his eyes blinking even more rapidly. "Me? Why would you ask?"

"Because you're an astute observer of people. You've probably taken traits from everyone involved in GK Productions and created new characters, in your mind, if not on paper."

A dull red crept up the back of his neck. Since his back hadn't been to the sun, Molly had to assume she'd guessed correctly and that he was embarrassed by her observation. "Maybe a little."

"Well, then? Anyone capable of murder?"

He considered the question thoughtfully. "Daniel has the temper for it," he said finally. "Laura's probably calculating enough. Duke might do it to protect himself. I don't know about the others."

"Veronica?"

"Not a chance," he said without hesitation. "She vents all her anger with words. She'd cut a man to ribbons with that sharp tongue of hers, but then she's ready to kiss and make up. She even sent a bottle of champagne to me after she publicly shredded a scene of mine day before yesterday."

Satisfied that his observations jibed with her own, Molly picked up the pace. Maybe the heat would sweat some of the alcohol out of the writer's system.

Minutes later, she delivered a reasonably sober Jonathan Fine to Laura. She felt almost guilty for doing it when Laura promptly began berating him. Jonathan pulled himself together sufficiently to defend the pages of script she wanted cut.

"Do you want this movie to make a bit of sense?" he finally snapped in exasperation.

"Of course, but we can handle some of this in cover shots, second unit stuff. We don't need dialogue."

"Maybe we should have hired a cast of mimes," Jonathan retorted.

From her place beside Jeannette, Molly cheered the return of his fighting spirit.

"You look pleased with yourself," Michael noted, coming up behind her.

"Just watching a shift in the balance of power."

"Laura Crain?"

"Yep."

"Who's that with her?"

"Jonathan Fine, the screenwriter. She's been giving him fits from the beginning, but today she seems even more tense than usual. Want me to introduce you, or would you rather wait for one of her better days?"

Michael watched Laura's tirade with evident fascination for several minutes. The look on his face might not have been so worrisome if Molly hadn't known how attracted he was to volatile women. During one unforgettable scene at the soccer field, she'd seen for herself how quickly Bianca's temper flared and how Michael had seemed to enjoy the passionate bout.

"Michael?"

"No, thanks. I'll introduce myself," he said and crossed the room.

Laura listened, her expression wary, as he showed her his badge. "I don't have time for this," she snapped.

"Make time," Michael countered in a friendly but adamant tone. He pulled up a chair.

Molly was prepared to gloat, but unfortunately Sergeant Jenkins arrived just in time to take the wind out of her sails.

"You and me," he said, gesturing toward the door. "Out there."

"We could talk here," Molly said hopefully. She wanted witnesses. Jenkins looked capable of a little police intimidation. He'd probably stop short of outright brutality.

He shook his head. "Now."

Molly followed him into the hallway. "I came straight down to the station when you called," she said hurriedly, hoping to forestall some of his anger. "You were just leaving."

"I know. I know. I saw you lurking around out there in the hall. Don't think I don't know who's responsible for getting O'Hara over here. Don't expect him to bail you out."

"I don't expect anything from him."

"Then maybe you'll explain to me what the hell you were doing at that motel on Eighth Street yesterday. Unless you're having an affair you're trying to keep secret, my guess is you were paying a call on one of my prime suspects. Why'd you go chasing after Francesca after I'd specifically told you to keep your nose out of this investigation?''

"You seem to know it all. Why bother asking me?"

"Because I want to make a point. I get very irritated when amateurs mess with my case. My ulcer starts acting up. There's not enough antacid on the face of the earth to make it quit, and that makes me cranky. When I get cranky, I start making calls. Official calls. Are you catching my drift here?''

"You'd like me to stay out of your way or you'll call my boss."

"You're mighty quick for a white girl."

"Could I ask one question before I go?"

"Certainly," he said magnanimously.

"Why is it that only one person in that motel room is on your list of suspects? The way I've got it figured, both of them have motive and opportunity."

His gaze narrowed. "Meaning?"

"Meaning Giovanni has an obsession with his star model and he was at the scene of the crime," she said. "I'm sure you'll follow up."

She left him with his mouth gaping and a murderous look in his weary, bloodshot eyes. He slammed his fist into the wall and took off for the stairwell. She had a hunch he was worried that he'd break her neck—to say nothing of several sections of the Florida criminal code—if he waited for the elevator.

• • •

"How are you and Sergeant Jenkins getting along?" Molly asked Michael that night. He had wangled a dinner invitation out of her late that afternoon. He'd brought along all the files on the case, probably just to remind her how much work she'd been responsible for having dumped in his lap. He'd also suggested she stop by the film office for her own file on Greg Kinsey and GK Productions. The file was crammed with publicity about the director and the film, along with copies of their shooting permits and schedules.

"Better than the two of you," he said. "He seems to find you worrisome."

"I'm sure you were able to commiserate with him on that score."

"I tried giving him some tips on handling you."

"Oh, really? How fascinating. Just when did you come up with these helpful hints?"

"About three days into that last case. I decided if I was going to survive with my sanity intact, I was going to have to find a way to work with you, instead of butting heads with you all the time."

"Which no doubt explains tonight's dinner invitation," she said wryly.

He smiled. "Exactly. You and I are going to discuss every single person involved in this case. You will offer your wisdom and insights. Then you will leave the rest to me."

"Happily."

His eyebrows lifted a fraction, but he refrained from comment.

Fortunately, Brian chose that moment to come

barreling through the front door with two of his friends. His blond hair was damp from a recent swim and his bare feet were covered with sand. "Hey, Mom, what's for dinner?"

"No 'Hello'? No 'How was your day, Mother?' " Molly inquired with a grin.

"Sorry, Mom. Did you catch any bad guys?"

Michael chuckled. "Maybe you ought to have a chat with your son about the exact nature of your job description."

She shot him a rueful look, then turned back to Brian. "You forgot the suntan lotion again, didn't you?"

He blinked and stared at her. "How'd you know?"

"Mothers know everything."

"Come on, really."

"Because you've got more freckles on your nose than you did when I saw you this morning. Now go out on the balcony and brush off the sand."

Brian glanced down as if the fine coating of sand had mysteriously appeared. He brushed at it.

"Brian, not in here!"

"Sorry." Brian poked Michael in the arm, then gazed at him hopefully. "You gonna stay for dinner?"

"That's the plan," Michael told him. "You guys been practicing your soccer?"

"Yeah. We'll be ready by Friday. Kevin's got an awesome move to show you."

"Awesome, huh? I can hardly wait."

Brian and his friends detoured to the balcony,

swiped at the sand, then went on to his room. Michael gazed after them. "You know how lucky you are?"

"Brian?"

"Yes. He's a great kid."

"I know it. Some days he's the only thing that gets me through." She regarded Michael oddly. "The way you feel about kids, I'm surprised you haven't gotten married and had a few of your own."

He shrugged. "It takes a lot to put up with the kind of lifestyle a cop has. I've never been willing to put any woman through that."

"I'm sure Bianca would have been more than willing."

"Maybe. It never came up," he said in a way that put an end to the conversation.

Since Molly was inclined to keep probing, it was probably just as well the phone rang.

"Mrs. DeWitt?"

"Yes."

"It's Jeffrey Meyerson."

His breathless tone immediately grabbed Molly's attention. "What's wrong, Mr. Meyerson?" she asked.

At her deliberate mention of Jeffrey's name, Michael glanced up from his stack of papers.

"It's Veronica," he said, sounding rattled. "She's been hurt."

"Hurt how? Was she in an accident?"

"She fell. They're taking her to the emergency room at Mount Sinai now. Can you meet us there?"

"Certainly. How badly is she hurt?"

"I think she's more shaken up than anything. It's not the fall I'm worried about."

"Oh?"

"I'm almost one hundred percent certain that she fell because someone shot at her."

CHAPTER
TWELVE

"Someone fired a shot at Veronica?" Molly repeated, dismay spreading through her. "Where? What happened? She wasn't hit, was she?"

Before Meyerson could provide any details, Michael had snatched the phone from her hands. She glared at him but retreated. This was his job, after all. At least the police angle belonged to him. Her job, in Vince's eyes anyway, probably included preventing incidents such as this.

With the incisiveness of an outstanding detective, Michael asked several terse questions. Unfortunately, Molly couldn't hear the replies, and Michael wasn't nearly as generous about repeating them aloud as she had been. Curiosity was killing her.

Five minutes later he hung up the phone, his expression grim. "Let's go."

Molly responded at once to the sense of urgency

in his tone. "Just let me see if Brian can go over to Kevin's for a while."

She made a quick call, then went through the apartment to get the boys from Brian's room. "I have to go out for a while. Kevin's mom said you can stay at their apartment until I get back. You'll have dinner there. Okay?"

"What's going on?" Brian said, looking from her to Michael and back again. "Another dead guy?"

He was clearly fascinated. The other two boys looked equally hopeful. They were at an age when the more gruesome something was, the better they liked it. She'd worried for a while that her precocious son's fascination with blood and gore was abnormal. After getting to know a few of his friends, however, she'd realized all eight-year-old boys were exactly alike.

Molly shook her head. "No, there is not another dead guy. There was an accident. Veronica Weston was hurt. We're going to the hospital to see her."

All three boys looked disappointed. They were only too ready to go to Kevin's.

As soon as she and Michael were on their way in his car, a mud-splattered wagon with soccer gear jumbled in the back, he said, "I'll drop you at the hospital. Then I want to swing back to the hotel and take a look at the scene."

Molly wasn't about to be left out of the search. She offered a more appealing alternative. "We could reverse that. I could look with you, then we could both go to the hospital."

"I thought Veronica would be your primary concern."

"She's okay. Meyerson said so. I'll do her more good if I can help find the person who fired the shot."

"If there was a shot."

Molly recognized the set to Michael's jaw. "You didn't believe him, did you?"

"I'm not sure. I believe she fell. I believe she probably even heard something. A shot? I don't know."

"Why would she say something like that, if it weren't true?"

"Publicity. Sympathy. Maybe to divert suspicion."

"Meaning?"

"If she could convince police that someone shot at her, then we'd have to accept the possibility that she's a potential victim, not a suspect. Carry that one step further and maybe the shot that killed Greg was actually meant for her. It would divert our attention from Kinsey's background."

Molly stared at him blankly. "Where'd that farfetched idea come from?"

"It's not so farfetched. It happened in her trailer. It was late at night. The shot was fired from some distance. Maybe all the killer saw was someone moving and fired before he or she realized it wasn't Veronica."

Molly considered Michael's unexpected theory. She turned to stare out at Biscayne Bay as they sped west across the Rickenbacker Causeway. The splashy setting sun had cast pink shadows on the water.

It had never occurred to her that Greg's death might have been accidental, that he might simply have been in the wrong place at the wrong time. Though Michael was right that it was possible, something about the theory didn't ring true.

"You say the shot was fired from a distance, right?"

"From outside the trailer anyway. Not from the steps or inside."

"So it would take a real marksman?"

He glanced over at her. "Probably. What's your point?"

"The bullet hit Greg in the middle of his forehead, didn't it?"

"Yes."

"Okay, say I'm a sharpshooter and I'm essentially firing at a shadowy figure. Wouldn't I be able to see that it was a man or a woman, or at least guess that from the height? Veronica's barely five feet three. Greg was six feet, maybe even an inch or two taller. Besides, wasn't the door open? No glass was broken. And the bullet was from a small-caliber gun. It wouldn't be accurate from any great distance, right?"

Michael grinned. "Exactly. You're starting to think like a cop."

Molly didn't waste time basking in the rare compliment. More concerned with the implication, she immediately asked, "Then we can rule out any kind of mistake in Greg's death?"

He shook his head. "You can't rule it out, but you can assume it's pretty damned unlikely."

Minutes later they had traveled back across Bis-

144

cayne Bay on the MacArthur Causeway, then straight east to Ocean Drive. Michael pulled into a parking space a block from the hotel.

"Where was Veronica when she heard the shot and fell?"

"From what Meyerson said, they'd been for a walk along the ocean. They had crossed the street and were about to go into the hotel."

"Did the shot come from behind them, in front of them, or from the side?"

"That's the problem. He has no idea."

"Then you can't actually expect to find a bullet out here."

Michael shrugged as he slammed the car door and locked it. "We can always try." He held out his hand. "Let's go."

Though the sun was rapidly sinking in the west, the summer night was still light enough for them to see clearly. Molly was all set to start searching the sidewalk on her hands and knees, but Michael headed straight into the hotel lobby and looked for the bell captain.

"I understand Ms. Weston took a fall outside the hotel tonight," he said. "Did you see it by any chance?"

The older Hispanic man—Rolando, according to his nametag—nodded. "*Sí!* I saw her."

"Can you show us?"

"*Sí!*" He hurried through the front door and led them to a spot in the middle of the sidewalk, just to the left of the entrance.

"Who called for an ambulance?" Molly asked.

The old man shook his head. "No ambulance. I

go inside to call right away, but the gentleman, he tells me 'No.' He say they will take a taxi to the hospital. Does this make sense? No. *Muy loco.*"

Molly shot a puzzled glance at Michael. "Why would he do that? I know he said she wasn't seriously injured, but wouldn't he want to be certain?"

"I guess that's something else we'll have to ask him," Michael replied. He turned back to the bellman. "Did you see anything else? Someone running away, perhaps? Someone who looked suspicious?"

"No, senor. Nothing. It is very quiet tonight. Very hot. People don't come so much, not until later."

"Any police around?"

The old man shook his head.

"Okay. *Gracias, amigo.*" When they were alone, Michael said, "Let's take a look around. It'll be like hunting for a needle in a haystack, but maybe we'll get lucky, if there really was a bullet."

They combed the sidewalk across the street, the paved roadway, the sidewalk in front of the hotel, even the front porch and the side of the building. There was no trace of a bullet or any mark that might have been left by one.

Michael finally gave up. "Let's get over to the hospital. When we get there, though, you go in and talk to Veronica, while I take Meyerson aside. I don't want them hearing what the other one's saying. We'll compare notes later."

Molly regarded him intently. "You still think Meyerson's mixed up in Greg's death, don't you? You think he invented this as some sort of smoke screen."

"Let's just say I've never been entirely satisfied with his explanation about his arrival in Miami and the length of time it took him to get to the hotel."

They drove into the parking lot at Mount Sinai, where the best view of Biscayne Bay was wasted on empty cars. In the emergency room Michael flashed his badge around and the triage nurse sent them back to the cubicle where Veronica was being treated.

The actress lay on a stretcher, looking a little wan, but otherwise fit. Not one hair was out of place. She took one look at Molly and demanded, "Can you spring me from this place? Jeffrey has this crazy notion that they should keep me overnight for observation. I absolutely refuse to spend one minute in one of those tacky, indecent hospital gowns."

"I think it makes sense, dear," Meyerson said, his tone placating. "You've had a terrible fright."

"Oh, for heaven's sakes, it's not as if anything dreadful happened," she said impatiently. "I fell. People stumble all the time."

Before Meyerson could respond, Michael took his arm and steered him out of the treatment area. "Why don't you explain what happened?" he suggested as he led the man away.

Molly stepped closer to the stretcher and took Veronica's hand. It was ice cold. She felt surprisingly frail. The actress's personality was so forceful, Molly had never really noticed until now just how petite she really was.

"How do you feel, really?" she asked when they were alone.

"I'm perfectly fine. Being thrown to the ground

like that was something of a shock, but aside from a couple of bruises, there's no damage done."

"Thrown to the ground," Molly repeated slowly. "I thought you fell."

"Jeffrey thought he heard a shot. He grabbed me and pushed me down, then fell on top of me. It was all terribly dramatic and dear of him, but to be perfectly honest, I think he was imagining things. Perhaps he felt guilty for not being here on Saturday and thought a rescue would salvage his pride."

"Then you didn't hear a shot?"

"I don't believe so. Of course, Jeffrey was awfully certain." Her brow creased with worried lines. "You don't suppose there really was a shot? Who on earth would want to kill me?"

Molly pulled a chair up beside her. "Let's think about that for a minute. Is there someone you don't get along with?"

"I suppose any number of people find me overbearing and demanding, but I don't think any of them would see that as grounds for murder. Even that Jonathan Fine person knows there's nothing personal in the things I say about his script. Everything I say is for the good of the film. I've had more experience than the whole bunch of them put together. Not that anyone asks my opinion."

She gave Molly a cheerful grin. "I suppose it's just as well that I'm not the kind of woman to wait to be asked, isn't it?"

Molly couldn't help laughing with her. Veronica had a certain indomitable spirit that she had to admire. No doubt that spirit had stood her in good stead as she'd battled her drinking problem.

Thinking of that, Molly reluctantly asked, "You hadn't been drinking or anything when you fell, had you?"

Veronica's expression turned sad. "I'm not surprised that you should ask about that, but no, I hadn't been drinking. Believe it or not, I do know my limits."

"Limits?"

Veronica sighed wearily. "Please, don't lecture. I've heard it all. No, I shouldn't touch a drop, but I seem to go for long periods when one or two drinks is plenty. Then something happens and, I don't know, I get crazy. One, two, ten drinks aren't enough. Do you know anything about alcoholics?"

Molly shook her head. "Not really, except some people should never take that first drink."

"And yet some of us have to, some of us need the booze to dull the pain."

As she spoke, a single tear tracked down her cheek. Molly had no doubt at all that it was genuine. Veronica's hand trembled in hers.

"Do you want to talk about it?"

With her free hand, Veronica reached for a tissue and wiped away the tear. She shook her head. "No. It's not something I can discuss. Not ever."

"Surely you talked about it with counselors when you were in that de-tox program."

"No. I couldn't even trust them with this. If it ever came out . . ." She sighed. "It simply can't and that's that."

Molly considered arguing with her, but she could see from Veronica's intractable expression that it would do little good. Whatever secret she had been hiding, for however long, was going to remain just that: her secret.

And her torment.

• • •

In the end, it was Michael who persuaded Veronica to remain hospitalized for the night. Molly wanted desperately to find out why he was so determined, but all she could do was to stand silently by as he cajoled until the actress finally said "Yes."

They stayed with her while she was taken to a VIP suite and settled in, then drove Jeffrey Meyerson back to the hotel.

"I suppose I must tell Ms. Crain what's happened," Meyerson said.

"Absolutely," Molly said. "It could affect tomorrow's shooting schedule, especially if she expected Veronica to be ready for an early makeup call. Would you like me to speak with her and explain that Veronica won't be available at least until midday?"

"Would you, my dear? That would be so helpful. This entire ordeal has exhausted me. And I must call Rome and explain that my arrival has been delayed."

"It must be the middle of the night there," Molly protested.

"My friends tend to party until the wee hours. I'm sure they will be awake. Even if they are not, they will forgive me when they hear what has happened to Veronica. She absolutely enchanted them when they visited Hollywood last winter."

"I'm not surprised," Michael said. "She's a charming woman. Have you known her long?"

"We met several years ago, under less than ideal circumstances. We knew immediately that we were kindred spirits."

"What were the circumstances?" Molly asked.

"It was one of those addiction treatment programs. She was trying to get off booze and I was having a little problem with some pain-killers my doctor had prescribed for a back problem."

"Then you didn't know Veronica from her film work?"

"I knew who she was, of course, but no, that was not a circle in which I traveled."

Molly promptly jumped to all sorts of conclusions that were based on Jeffrey Meyerson's explanation and her own growing distrust of the man. He was too polished, too slippery. And for some reason he had lied about Veronica's hearing the shot. It might have been a minor discrepancy in their stories, but it also might be an indication that there had been no shot at all.

Why, though? What did Jeffrey Meyerson have to gain by setting up some fake rescue attempt? Molly's best guess wasn't particularly flattering. Chances were he was a man who'd seen Veronica as a meal ticket and latched on for the ride. He certainly seemed to make more of their relationship than the actress had actually admitted to. Veronica had never confirmed that there was any engagement.

"What about Greg Kinsey?" Michael asked. "Did you know him?"

Meyerson shook his head. "Never met the man. I wish I had. From everything I've heard, he was a great talent. What a shame to lose him before he could do his greatest work."

He sounded sincere enough. Molly wondered, though, if the extraordinarily protective Meyerson had found Greg's treatment of Veronica too demeaning. Would he have seen that as grounds for murder?

At the hotel, he hurried off to his room and Molly made a quick call to Laura's room. The producer wasn't in, so she left a message with Jerry Shaw.

"Is that going to foul up the morning schedule too badly?" she asked.

"I don't think so. We can juggle a couple of scenes. Shoot around Veronica, then do her pickups when she gets here."

"Terrific. Thanks, Jerry. I'll see you in the morning."

When she'd hung up, she found Michael on a pay phone across the lobby. "Yeah, that's right. Meyerson, Jeffrey, and Weston, Veronica. Do what you can for me and fax it, okay? Thanks."

"Who were you calling?" Molly asked.

"An investigator I know in L.A. He owes me a favor. He'll dig around a little and see what he can come up with."

"Is he checking on anyone else?"

"Not yet. He's been working on Kinsey a couple of days, but he hasn't come up with anything much beyond his official bio. The guy wasn't mixed up in anything illegal or, if he was, his record had been wiped clean."

"How about GK Productions? Can he take a look at how the company was set up?"

"Why?"

"I'm just curious about what happens now that Greg's dead. I know Daniel owns a piece of the company, but I'm not sure about Hank and Laura. They may have been employees or they could be co-owners. It would make a difference when it comes to motive."

Michael nodded and reached for the phone. "Les, it's me again. Check into a film company for me, while you're at it. GK Productions. I need to know the setup. Who gets it with Greg dead? Who owns a piece? Yeah, a GK Productions without GK doesn't make much sense to me either, but who knows. There's a Daniel Ortiz, who reportedly owns a chunk. He's the director of photography on this picture, probably on all Kinsey's other films as well. Listen, if you come up with anything tonight, I'll be at this number for the next couple of hours or you can try my beeper, if that number doesn't answer."

He reeled off Molly's home number, then hung up.

"And just why wouldn't my number answer?" Molly asked.

"Because it's ten o'clock at night and I'm starved. Even working cops get to eat once in a while."

"There's food at home. I just need to heat it up."

"Nope. Your day's been just as long as mine. Let's go for Cuban."

Molly tried to hide her surprise at the offer to take her onto his turf. She was even more surprised when she realized the tiny Little Havana restaurant was owned by an uncle, who greeted Michael boisterously, seated them with a flourish at a formica-topped counter, then brought them huge platters of *palomilla* steak smothered in onions, along with black beans and rice and sweet, fried plantains.

Tio Pedro, his pristine white apron stretched taut over an impressive belly, his black hair shot through with gray, and his black eyes alive with laughter, stood over them as they ate. He nodded approvingly as Michael finished every bite on his plate, then polished off her leftovers.

"Where you been?" he demanded of Michael when he was satisfied that his nephew would not starve to death. "Elena and me, we not see you for two, maybe three weeks now."

"Working, Tio. You know how it goes."

"Not working too hard to have dinner with a pretty woman, I see. Your mama has met the senorita?"

Michael chuckled. "You ask too many questions, Tio. You are embarrassing Molly."

Tio Pedro didn't look the least bit contrite. "You bring her for Sunday dinner. I invite the whole family."

Molly held her breath, waiting for Michael's reply. She had no doubt that Sunday dinner was a major event in his large Cuban family. To be asked was probably significant, something reserved for a girl friend of some importance.

Michael looked at her. "What about it? You feel like braving the inquisition? You can bring Brian."

Trying to match his casual note, she nodded. "Sure. Sounds like fun."

Michael chuckled at that. "Fun is not the way I would describe one of the family get-togethers, especially when you are on display."

"Display?"

"To see if you are suitable for the most eligible bachelor in the family."

"I don't suppose you'd like to give me odds on getting a satisfactory approval rating."

He winked. "I wouldn't worry about it. My opinion is the only one that counts."

CHAPTER
THIRTEEN

Less than seventy-two hours after the death of Greg Kinsey, the entire cast and crew, with the exception of the still-hospitalized Veronica, assembled at the same oceanfront location where the murder had taken place. The production trailer was parked on the same side street. Veronica's impounded trailer had been replaced by one slightly smaller awaiting her arrival. Duke Lane's trailer with its special dark-tinted windows had been parked around the corner. Despite the brilliant glare of the sun on sand and sea, the vibes were very dark.

Molly found Laura Crain and Hank Murdock in the production trailer just after eight A.M. They were already immersed in a stack of script pages with little yellow flags marking key sections scheduled for filming that morning.

"We'll finish up here by one o'clock and break for lunch," Laura was saying. "Then I want everything set up in that fake fishing village over on Virginia Key no later than two.''

Hank was already shaking his head. "It won't work, not unless Veronica gets here before noon. I can't get her shots done in an hour. She has three pages of dialogue in that scene with Duke. You know damn well she'll never get it in one or two takes. She'll probably spend that long arguing with Jonathan about her lines. Is he on the set, by the way? We can't waste time chasing him down every time she complains. I want him in here all day."

Laura nodded. "I'll take care of it." She glanced at Molly. "Think you could get him for me?"

Molly reached for a cellular phone.

"I said *get him,* not call him," Laura snapped.

Molly considered reminding the producer that she was not her errand girl, but decided it wouldn't accomplish a thing. Laura seemed to consider everyone connected with the film, with the possible exception of Hank, and before him Greg, as her personal lackey. After listening to Laura tell Hank what to do just now, Molly wasn't sure the hapless director didn't fall into the same category.

"Stress," she mumbled under her breath as she shut the trailer door behind her. Everyone on the set was bound to be under incredible stress this morning. Between the murder itself and anxiety over Hank's ability to fill Greg's shoes, it was no wonder everyone was edgy. By afternoon, she hoped, things would settle down or there could well be another murder on the set.

Molly was halfway back to the hotel when to her

absolute astonishment she spotted Vince coming toward her. The last time her boss had actually bothered dropping by a film on location in south Florida, the star had been the previous month's *Playboy* centerfold. They couldn't have ejected him from that set with dynamite. Usually he preferred golfing with the studio execs or ogling the starlets at the lively wrap parties that concluded the film company's stay in south Florida.

"What brings you by?" she inquired warily. He was actually wearing a jacket, formal attire for a man who preferred lime-green golfing pants and knit shirts in a rainbow of pastels.

"Politics," he said in a rare display of total honesty. "I figured I'd better try to smooth things over, offer my condolences, et cetera. Where are you headed?"

"Laura just sent me in search of the screenwriter. They want him on standby."

"She's in the production trailer?"

"With Hank. She should be trying to bolster his self-confidence. Instead, she seems intent on making him panic over the shooting schedule. If I were Hank, I'd tell her to get the hell back to the hotel and stay there. He won't do it though. Maybe you can get her out of there."

Vince regarded her blankly. "How?"

"I'm not suggesting you use your usual technique. You don't need to seduce her. Just ask to meet everyone. Play the role of local dignitary to the hilt. You can ooze charm when you want to."

Her boss seemed to consider that a compliment. He waved distractedly as he marched off to impress

Laura Crain. He was obviously completely confident he could do it.

Molly found Jonathan Fine in his room, still half asleep. To answer her knock he'd dragged on a pair of pants for decency's sake, but wore no shirt. He was so thin she could practically count his ribs.

"Hank needs you on the set," she told him.

Without his glasses, the writer squinted at her. "Molly?"

"Yes."

"I was up most of the night making the changes Laura wanted. Does he need me now?"

"He says he does."

Jonathan sighed heavily. "Wait a sec. I'll come with you. See if room service can bring up a pot of very strong coffee on the double."

Molly nodded and made the call while Jonathan retreated to the bathroom to shower. He emerged in minutes, wearing shorts and yet another brilliantly flowered shirt. His glasses were in place, but his eyes still looked vague. He hadn't shaved and a faint stubble shadowed his jaw.

"Coffee?" he murmured desperately, blinking at her.

"On its way."

"Thank God." He sank down on the side of the bed to wait.

"You worked all night?"

"Until five this morning. What time is it?"

"Eight twenty."

"Shit."

"Was it just last night's hours or are you not a morning person?"

"Mornings are fine. I just prefer six or seven hours of sleep before they arrive."

A tap on the door announced the arrival of the coffee. Jonathan gratefully drank down an entire cup, poured a second cup and said, "Let's do it. I should live."

They got back to the location just in time to hear Laura scream, "I want you off of this set. Now! Am I making myself clear?"

Molly was about to run to Vince's rescue, but it seemed the person Laura was dismissing so summarily was Michael. It didn't seem like the best approach to take with the policeman in charge of investigating Greg's murder. Michael, however, actually looked amused.

"Sorry. I'm here for the duration," he told her. "I have statements I need to go over with some of your people."

"Not in the middle of production, you don't," Laura shouted. "Do I need to call the mayor of this goddamn town to get you out of here?"

"You can call anyone you want. I'm staying. Maybe we should start with your statement," he suggested pleasantly. "That way your crew can get to work."

It was the best suggestion Molly had heard all morning, but Laura apparently didn't see it that way. She was still making noises about reporting Michael to every official from the mayor to the governor. Molly was surprised she left out the President of the United States.

"That does my heart good," Jonathan said as

they watched Michael depart with his reluctant witness. "It almost makes getting up worthwhile."

"I know what you mean," Molly said, wondering where Vince had gone since he obviously wasn't with Laura.

He turned up just as she found a place behind the cables where she could watch Duke Lane shoot his first scene of the day.

"Thanks a lot," he muttered in her ear.

"For what?"

"Sending me in to see that woman without a rabies shot. She's a viper."

"Your charm failed you?"

"A dozen bottles of champagne couldn't mellow her out. Why'd Kinsey put up with her?"

"Word was he was sleeping with her."

Vince shook his head in bemusement. "He was a braver man than I."

Considering Vince's enthusiastic pursuit of a wide range of women, Molly considered that high praise for Kinsey or a damning indictment of Laura. Probably a little of each.

"Quiet on the set," Hank finally shouted. He glanced at Daniel Ortiz, who nodded. "Roll film." He gestured toward Duke Lane. "And action."

The scene required a highly emotional delivery, one of the toughest to begin cold, especially with a stand-in substituting for the missing Veronica. Duke never faltered. A tense three minutes later, when Hank said, "Cut and print," the crew burst into applause.

"He's good," Vince said, sounding astonished.

"To be perfectly honest, he was better this

morning than I've ever seen him. I have a hunch Veronica and her tantrums make him nervous."

"He actually said his lines the way I wrote them," Jonathan said, his tone suggesting amazement.

While he waited for Hank and Daniel to set up for his next shot, Duke made his way over to Molly, Vince, and Jonathan.

"Good changes," he told Jonathan.

"You were really on this morning," the writer told him. "Too bad Veronica missed it."

"She would have hated it," Duke said ruefully. "She likes to step all over my lines. Watch when we shoot her angles later. She'll be all over the place."

"Didn't Greg try to control her?"

"Greg thought she walked on water," Duke said. "Don't ask me why. She treated him the way Laura treats all the rest of us, like dirt."

"Taking my name in vain?" Veronica inquired, strolling up in the middle of his comment. Jeffrey Meyerson, looking distressed, was at her side.

"Now, dear," he said soothingly. "Don't get upset."

"Oh, shut up, Jeffrey," she said.

Duke met Veronica's gaze evenly and didn't waste his breath offering an apology. After a beat, she actually winked at him and the tension snapped.

Molly studied her closely. "You're okay?"

"Fine," the actress said. "Jeff, go find the makeup girl and tell her I'm here. Molly, could you be a dear and let Hank know?" She gestured to Jonathan. "Bring along the new pages. We can go over them while they're working on my hair and makeup.''

"Certainly," the writer said, looking miserable.

Hank came over just in time to hear the exchange. "No changes, Veronica. We're shooting this the way Jonathan wrote it. Duke's already done his angle.''

Veronica responded to the challenge in Hank's tone with a terse "We'll see."

"I told you," Duke mumbled, following Hank back to the set.

Hank draped an arm over Duke's shoulder and leaned close. Whatever he was telling the actor so intensely seemed to relax him. Duke was smiling when he stepped back in front of the camera. Daniel shot him a thumbs-up as Hank called for action to begin again.

"How's Hank doing?" Michael whispered to Molly as he joined her.

She raised her finger to her lips. Michael waited impatiently for the next break in filming when she was finally able to speak. "He's in control so far. Better than I expected, in fact. If Veronica's on good behavior, this may go smoothly."

"You idiot!" Veronica's shout couldn't have been timed more perfectly if Jonathan himself had scripted it. "Are you trying to ruin me?"

Hank and Molly started for Veronica's trailer just in time to see a furious Jonathan Fine storm through the door. "Keep her away from me," he said to Hank. "If you need me, I'll be back at the hotel."

"I need you here," Hank pleaded. "Wait in the production trailer."

Jonathan ran his hand through his hair but finally nodded. "One word from her, though, and I'm on the next plane out of here. I don't care if I never sell another script."

Molly rushed up the steps to Veronica's trailer. Inside she found the actress surrounded by a hair stylist, a makeup artist, and a frantic Jeffrey Meyerson. She was looking rather pleased with herself.

"What on earth did you say to Jonathan?" Molly asked her.

"I told him this was my film, not Duke Lane's, and that he'd better not forget it." She picked up the new script pages from her dressing table and dumped them into the trash for emphasis. Molly winced.

"They're just tightening up a few scenes to speed up production. They were probably making a few adjustments just in case you couldn't get here today."

"Bullshit. Now that Laura's in charge, she wants to turn this into Duke's film. If I have to call my agent and get him involved, then that's what I'll do."

Hank sighed heavily. "Okay, everyone out of here," he said. "Veronica and I need to talk."

When Jeffrey stayed where he was, Hank said, "You, too, Meyerson. Molly, I'd like you to stay."

The only reason Molly could think of for being included was Hank's belief that she had a soothing effect on his temperamental star. Personally, she would have rather been in Siberia. She thought Veronica was behaving like a spoiled brat and wasn't sure she wouldn't tell her as much given another display of her lousy temper.

When everyone else had left, Hank sat across from Veronica.

"You know we have a problem here," he said.

She nodded. "I'll say."

"You're not helping," he said flatly. "You can make or break this film. It's your choice. Now, me, I think this can be the best thing you've ever done, but you have to trust me."

Some of Veronica's defensiveness faded. "Explain," she said imperiously.

"You dominate every scene in which you appear. What does it matter if Duke has a few more lines? He's playing to you. There will never be a question of who this picture belongs to. You have star billing. This is not some cameo appearance. You carry it. It would make life a lot easier if you'd give Duke and Jonathan a break. You have them so terrified the only time I get any decent work out of either of them is when you're not around."

Veronica looked stunned by Hank's frank assessment of her effect on the others. "I just want this to be a great film."

"That's what we all want. If you'd spend half as much energy in front of the camera as you do off-screen, there wouldn't be a star in Hollywood who could hold a candle to you."

Veronica blossomed visibly under Hank's deft praise. Molly silently applauded. He seemed to know exactly how to appeal to her sense of vanity. Veronica would not want it known around Hollywood that she and she alone had turned yet another film into a disaster.

"You're quite a flatterer, Mr. Murdock," Veronica said, bestowing one of her most brilliant smiles on him. "I think I could learn to adore you. Now let's get this show under way."

Hank grinned back at her. "Thank you. I'll send Jerry for you when we're ready."

Molly wondered if Veronica noticed his sigh of relief as he exited the trailer.

"You old fraud," Molly said, when they were alone. "You knew from the minute he walked in here you were going to do as he asked, didn't you?"

"It never hurts to remind everyone of who I am," Veronica said, fluffing her chestnut hair until it fell into its usual sensuous waves. "Of course, I still think Duke Lane is an impertinent twit who's trying to steal this picture."

"The better he looks, the better you look," Molly reminded her. "If the audience doesn't love him, they're going to think you're the twit for chasing after him."

Veronica's brow knit as she considered Molly's analysis. "You have a point, my dear. Tell Duke I'd like to see him. Perhaps we can put this rivalry to rest."

Molly wasn't so sure that was the best idea she'd heard all day, but she left to follow the actress's instructions. She ran into Michael just outside the door.

"I thought maybe she'd taken you apart in there," he said.

"I notice you didn't rush in to my rescue."

"Last I heard, you preferred to stand up for yourself."

Molly didn't bother to respond to that. "She wants to see Duke. Think I dare send him in?"

"You know her mood better than I do. I can always stand guard."

"Probably not a bad idea."

Molly found Duke hiding out in his own trailer. "Veronica wants to see you."

He drew his sunglasses down just low enough to peer at her over the top rim. "You're kidding me."

"Nope. She wants to make amends."

He looked even more disbelieving, but he settled his glasses back into place and followed Molly back to Veronica's trailer. He rapped on the door and stepped inside.

Molly and Michael lingered just outside. Just when Molly was convinced that things had to be going smoothly, she heard Veronica's voice climb.

"Don't you threaten me," Duke countered just as loudly. "Push me too hard and I'll tell everyone what I know about you and Greg Kinsey."

"You bastard," Veronica said in a low tone that Molly and Michael heard only because Michael had yanked open the door about two seconds before.

He stepped inside and looked from Duke's angry face to the flaming pink in Veronica's cheeks. "Maybe you'd better tell me what you know," he said quietly to Duke.

Veronica looked shaken. She stared at Duke intently, her expression pleading. He muttered an oath under his breath, then met Michael's gaze evenly.

"I don't know a thing," he said flatly. "I was just blowing off steam."

"That's not the way it sounded."

Duke shrugged. "I'm a hell of an actor."

Molly and Michael both looked from Duke to Veronica and back again. There wasn't a doubt in Molly's mind that Duke was lying through his teeth, but short of hooking him up to a lie detector and questioning him from now till dusk, she couldn't see any way of getting him to say anymore.

Veronica, on the other hand, looked as if she'd crack if they asked her anything more consequential than her name. Molly couldn't help wondering why.

CHAPTER
FOURTEEN

Hank saved Veronica from having to say another incriminating word at that moment. He called for both the actress and Duke Lane to shoot their critical farewell scene. Given the high emotions off the set, they should radiate tension on screen.

"The minute you've finished, you and I are going to have a little chat," Michael told the actress as she practically bolted from the trailer.

She glanced toward Molly with a look of pure desperation, but Molly could only shrug. When Michael wanted to question a murder suspect, she could hardly intervene. As much as she didn't want to believe that Veronica had anything at all to do with Greg's death, she had no evidence to prove it. As far as she knew, Michael had no evidence to prove otherwise, but then that was exactly what he was hoping to discover in that interrogation.

In front of the camera Veronica's nervousness

was unmistakable, even worse than it had been on the first day of shooting when everyone knew how much was at stake for her in this film.

She blew her first, simple line half a dozen times. Hank spoke to her with incredible patience. Even Duke himself sought to soothe her nerves by taking her aside and whispering to her. She smiled shakily at him, but couldn't hide the worried, distrustful look in her eyes.

Even so, on the next take, she delivered the lines—all three pages' worth—flawlessly. It was a bravura performance under the tense conditions. This time, when Hank called "Cut," the crowd gathered around the perimeter applauded. Duke took Veronica's hand and kissed it with a dramatic flourish. Clearly flustered by the gesture, she met his gaze. Whatever she saw there must have reassured her because she walked toward Molly and Michael with a renewed spring in her step and a confident set to her shoulders.

"Come along," she said to them. "You can ride over to Virginia Key with me. Jeffrey should have luncheon waiting in the trailer."

Indeed the small, damask-covered table was set with expensive silver, crystal, and china. Champagne cooled in a bucket and a colorful fruit salad rested on iced plates. Jeffrey welcomed them as if the luncheon were being served in some elegant dining room rather than in a made-over recreational trailer that had been hurriedly spruced up for Veronica's temporary use. He'd even added a bouquet of yellow roses, reportedly the actress's favorite. Veronica said nothing about his efforts. She seemed to take them as her due.

As the trailer left Miami Beach to go to the Virginia Key location, Michael asked Veronica what Duke had been talking about when he'd threatened her earlier.

"After lunch," she said insistently. "We shouldn't let all this lovely food go to waste."

"And after lunch, you'll use the next scene as an excuse," Michael said. "Why don't you just tell me whatever you know now? Get it over with so you don't ruin your digestion."

Since no one was eating the beautifully displayed meal, Molly thought worrying about the star's enjoyment of it was wasted effort.

Veronica finally lifted her gaze until she was staring straight into Michael's eyes. "I don't know anything," she said, her voice steady.

"You're saying Duke was lying earlier, that his threat meant nothing?"

"That's what I'm telling you."

Despite Veronica's sincere delivery, not even Molly believed her. Michael tried another tack. "Tell me about your relationship with Kinsey."

"He had a reputation as a hot director. We didn't always agree. We argued quite a bit, in fact. I'm sure everyone has told you that already."

"When did you meet?"

"When he contacted me about starring in this movie. Our agents arranged a breakfast meeting at the Beverly Hills Hotel." She glanced at Molly. "You must let me take you there the next time you fly out to L.A. The place raises the concept of power break-fasts to new heights."

"Did you and Kinsey get along then?" Michael persisted.

"It was a pleasant breakfast. I believe I had fresh strawberries."

Molly seriously doubted Michael was interested in the menu. Even so, he inquired pleasantly, "And Mr. Kinsey?"

"Melon, as I recall. Eggs Benedict. I told him he was probably killing himself with all that choles-terol."

"I'm sure he appreciated your concern," Michael retorted dryly, just as his beeper went off. He glanced at the calling number, then reached for the cellular phone he'd been carrying around on loca-tion.

"O'Hara," he said tersely once the call went through. He listened intently. The rest of them sat around watching him. Jeffrey tried to break the silence, but Veronica cut him off with a look.

"Okay, got it," Michael said. "You'll fax the rest to the office? Right. I'll call if I need anything else. Thanks."

All three of them watched him expectantly. He foiled them all by returning at once to that long-ago breakfast at the Polo Lounge of the Beverly Hills Hotel.

"What was your impression of Greg when you met him?"

"He was a pleasant young man," Veronica said. "What more can I say? You can't tell how talented someone is just by talking with them. I screened sev-

eral of his films later that same day. Those told the
story. This was someone I knew I should work with.
The clippings my agent gave me about his background and successes intrigued me.''

"Did he explain to you why he was so intent on
casting you in this picture?''

She hesitated, then said, ''No. I assumed he simply thought I was right for the role.''

"Surely other actresses would have been equally
right. Good roles for women your age are tough to
come by. Competition must have been fierce.''

"It may have been. I can't really say. To my
knowledge I was the only one Greg ever considered.''

"Why?'' Michael repeated.

"Greg is the only one who could answer that.''

"Unfortunately, he's dead.''

Veronica blinked rapidly at Michael's harsh
tone. ''I think we're all very much aware of that,
Detective.''

"But you don't seem nearly as concerned about
finding his killer as I am. Why won't you tell me
what Duke was talking about?''

"I can't,'' she said, her eyes suddenly welling
with unshed tears. If it was a deliberate play for sympathy, it didn't work.

"Can't or won't?'' he asked, hammering at her.
No one had touched a bite of the food on the table.
If Molly's was any example, their stomachs were all
tied in knots.

"I don't know,'' Veronica swore. ''I'm telling
you the truth, Detective. I don't know what Duke
Lane knows or thinks he knows.''

Michael muttered an oath and sat back. "Okay. We'll save it for later."

Jeffrey Meyerson scowled at him. "Really, I must protest. Can't you see how your questions are upsetting her?"

"I'm trying to conduct a murder investigation. People tend to get upset now and then. If Ms. Weston has nothing to hide, then my questions shouldn't distress her."

"Your tone would distress Attila the Hun," Molly mumbled just loud enough for him to hear her clearly. He reached over and circled her wrist with his hand. He applied just enough pressure to warn her to keep her smart remarks to herself.

The minute the trailer pulled into the road to Virginia Key and the quaint, colorful fishing village that had been constructed for use as a working film set, Veronica practically ran in search of Hank. It was the first time she'd ever been on the set before her call.

Michael stood in the doorway and watched her go.

"Are you satisfied?" Molly demanded. "You were actually cruel in there."

"I was doing my job," he retorted, lifting his sunglasses so she couldn't miss the banked fury in his eyes. "And the next time you decide to interfere, I'll charge you with obstruction of justice."

Molly gaped at him. "You're serious, aren't you?"

"You're damned right. I wanted to put the fear of God into her in there. She knows something and

I want to know what. With you and Meyerson rushing to her defense, she squirmed off the hook."

"She's a human being, dammit. Not some fish you're trying to reel in."

"She is a murder suspect," he said flatly. "Maybe the best one we've got."

"She didn't do it," Molly countered.

"Thank you for your unbiased, fact-based opinion," he snapped. "Now, if you'll excuse me, I'll get over to headquarters so I can take a look at the reports Les just faxed to me."

"How are you going to get back?"

"Unless I miss my guess, Otis Jenkins followed us over here in his car. He'll take me. I think he'll be very interested in what Les has to say about your innocent star."

Before Molly could demand to know what he meant by that, he'd crossed the street and climbed into Jenkins's unmarked car, which was indeed waiting.

Molly stared after them as the car's tires spun on the dirt shoulder before making a U-turn and heading out at a speed a good twenty miles an hour over the limit. Molly hoped they bounced over a speed bump at that pace and had some sense knocked into their hard heads.

• • •

If Veronica Weston refused to answer Michael's questions, there was one other person who had the same information, Molly realized as she brushed away yet another mosquito. After days of rain and weeks of still, hot, humid air, the pesky insects had multiplied into irritating swarms. The production assistant with the can of bug spray was the most popular man on the set.

Duke Lane had raised the issue of some secret he and Greg Kinsey had shared involving Veronica. Molly had no doubt that his quick denial had been a lie. She walked down the dirt path from the set until she located his trailer parked in the scant shade offered by a row of Australian pines.

Duke's terse "Yes" was all she got in response to her knock. She opened the trailer door and stepped inside, savoring the dark interior and chill air. A flute sonata that Molly recognized as Mozart's played softly.

The actor was lounging back in a padded swivel chair, his feet propped on an ice chest. His hands were folded in his lap. A dog-eared, open book lay on his chest. Thoreau's *Walden*. She would have considered it an odd choice had she not read that he was among those fighting to save the lovely, historic pond and its serene surrounding forest from developers.

Molly couldn't tell if Duke's eyes were open or not. Despite the dim lighting, he was wearing his sunglasses.

"We need to talk," she said, taking the chair opposite him.

"About cabbages and kings?"

"About Greg Kinsey and Veronica Weston."

"Sorry. No can do."

"Why not? You obviously know something. Veronica's terrified."

Duke whipped off his glasses, lowered his feet to

the floor and leaned forward, his expression intent. "You know the hell of it? I really did throw that comment out just to see what happened. I really don't know a damned thing. I just picked up on some weird vibes about those two over the last few weeks. I took a chance that my observation would shake Veronica enough to get her to cooperate in that last scene. I was as stunned as anybody when she reacted the way she did."

"I don't believe you."

"It's the truth."

"Okay, let's talk about those vibes, then. What did you see or think you saw?"

"You want a beer?"

Molly shook her head. He opened the cooler, withdrew a light beer in a glass bottle, and popped off the cap. After he'd taken a long, slow swallow, he sat back in his chair.

"I guess it started with the way Greg watched her. I mean the woman's a beauty, especially for someone her age, but Greg always had this slightly awestruck look on his face. You know what I mean?"

"Not really," Molly admitted. "Maybe he'd always admired her films and was thrilled to be working with her."

Duke considered the explanation. "Oh, there was some of that. No doubt about it. But this was something else, something personal."

"Are you saying he was attracted to her? It wouldn't be the first time an older woman appealed to a younger man."

"Hell, no. Greg had a type. Dark-haired, thin to the point of emaciation. Like Laura and that Italian

model he fell for. He also liked to play the role of
mentor, liked the adoration. Veronica doesn't fit
into that mold at all. She seemed to appreciate his
talent, but she certainly wasn't in awe of him."

"Are you saying this feeling, whatever it was, was
more on Greg's side than on Veronica's?"

He hesitated before answering. "Yeah. I think it
was."

"How well did you know Greg?"

"Professionally. We didn't socialize, either before production started or since. We have different
agendas."

"Meaning he chases women and you don't,"
Molly suggested with as much subtlety as she could
manage.

Duke grinned ruefully. "You can say it, Molly.
I'm gay. It's not something I bother to hide. People
can accept me or not. My agent says I'm nuts to go
public. He thinks it'll hurt me in the long run, but
so far I've done okay. I don't regret being so
straightforward about my sexuality."

"You tried to hide it when we were with Michael
the other day. You referred to your squeeze several
times in a way that implied it was a woman."

He shrugged. "Cops make me nervous."

"You guessed he was a cop? He hadn't even
been assigned to the case at that point."

"Observing people is what makes a good actor.
I know all the signs. Besides, he had too many questions for some casual acquaintance of yours. I figured I'd play out the scene and see what happened."

"Okay, since you know, then you probably also know he wondered if you had a thing for Greg."

"So he said. I didn't. Why waste energy on something that can't be?"

"But there is someone here with you? A man?"

Duke nodded. "Don't bother trying to speculate. He's not on the film, not even in the business."

"But he is your alibi for Saturday night when Greg was shot. Have you told Michael about him?"

"O'Hara has all the information he needs to conclude that I wasn't anywhere near Miami Beach at the time Greg died. I'm sure he's checked it out. He strikes me as a pretty thorough guy."

Molly nodded. "Which means if you are lying about what you know about Veronica and Greg, he'll find out. He won't be happy that you've withheld information."

"Do you believe me?"

She gazed into his guileless eyes and decided that whatever else Duke Lane might skirt the truth about, he wasn't lying about this. On some things she simply had to go with her instincts, and he had convinced her.

"Yes," she told him finally. "I believe you. But if you think of anything else, anything that might explain these feelings of yours about the two of them, will you pass it along?"

"To you or the cop?"

"I have a hunch the cop would prefer it if you gave the information to him firsthand." She grinned. "I wouldn't mind hearing it second, though."

Duke nodded. "That's a promise, then."

She glanced at the table and spotted a cellular phone. "Mind if I make a call?"

"Be my guest."

She dialed Liza. "I need another favor," she said, when she got her. "I'm stranded out here on Virginia Key and I need to get over to the Beach. Can you pick me up and give me a lift to the police station over there?"

"A break in the case?"

"Could be. Michael's friend in L.A. picked up on something and he's checking it out now. He wouldn't tell me before he left here."

"What'd you do to tick him off? Meddle in his investigation?"

"Something like that."

"And you're on your way to do more meddling?"

"Only if you'll come get me. Otherwise I'll be stuck over here dying of curiosity."

"Where are you exactly?"

Molly described the location and Duke's trailer.

"Can I meet him?" Liza asked. "We've crossed paths at a couple of these big environmental fundraisers, but we've never met. I'd like to tell him how much I admire his idealism."

"If you get here before Hank calls him to the set, I'm sure Duke would be happy to hear he has yet another fan."

"On my way."

Duke's gaze had narrowed at Molly's end of the conversation. "Not some teenybopper? You wouldn't do that to me."

"Actually this fan admires your mind. She's tackling the rain forest this month."

Duke sank back in his chair and replaced his sunglasses. "Call me when she gets here. I'm gonna meditate."

The hum of the air-conditioner had almost lulled Molly to sleep in the couple of minutes it took Liza to arrive. She and Duke compared notes on the environment, mutual friends, and the ozone layer while Molly stared longingly at Liza's car.

"Why doesn't your friend just hang out here with me?" Duke finally suggested. "If she doesn't mind lending you her car, that is. I'll give her a lift home later."

Liza tossed the keys to Molly in mid-sentence. "I guess that's a 'Yes,' " Molly concluded. "I don't suppose either of you has a theory about how I should get my own car back to Key Biscayne later?"

"Have the hunk drive it," Liza said.

"The hunk?" Duke repeated with evident fascination.

"Never mind," Molly said hurriedly. "I'll work it out."

If the look on Michael's face when he and Jenkins tore away an hour before was any indication, she doubted she could count on *the hunk* for much of anything at the moment.

CHAPTER
FIFTEEN

Before heading back to Miami Beach, Molly decided to make a quick run home to check on Brian. Although Kevin's mom looked after both boys during the summer, she worried about his becoming in essence a latchkey kid. Fortunately, Brian had become a favorite of Nestor, the condo's head of security. He was a former Nicaraguan Freedom Fighter, and she knew no harm would come to her son as long as Nestor was on duty.

She pulled up in the circular drive in front of the building and parked the car. Nestor greeted her with a worried look and a barrage of Spanish. The only word she understood clearly was *esposo*.

"Whose husband?" she demanded of the obviously distressed guard. "Not mine? Here?"

"*Sí, sí,*" Nestor said. "Senor DeWitt. *Aquí.*"

"Oh, dear Lord," Molly said and took off at a run. What was Hal up to now?

Upstairs she found her son planted on the sofa. A stubborn, sullen expression on his face exactly matched that on his father's. Hal was pacing, his long angry strides taking him from living room to dining room, from the front door to the balcony's sliding glass doors.

"Brian, go to your room, please," Molly said, every muscle in her body tied in knots.

He didn't waste a second complying, which told her just how tense things had been before her arrival.

"What are you doing here, Hal?" she said quietly, determined to fight the urge to scream at him at the top of her lungs.

He glared at her belligerently. "I came to see my son."

"Why were the two of you arguing if it was as simple as that?"

"He wanted me to leave with him," Brian said from the hallway. Obviously he'd never made it all the way to his room.

"Okay, Brian, leave us alone now, will you?"

He looked undecided.

"It's okay," she told him. "I promise."

As soon as she was certain he had finally gone, she whirled on Hal. "Don't you ever, *ever* do something like this again. If I have to I'll go to court, have our custody agreement invalidated, and get a restraining order against you."

"You weren't here. What the hell difference does it make to you if I spend a few extra hours with my son?"

Molly took a deep breath and tried to calm

down. "If I thought for one minute that was all you'd intended, I would be delighted. Brian would be thrilled."

"What makes you think it was anything more?" he said sullenly.

"The fact that you came roaring in here on Sunday threatening to take him away. The fact that you usually cancel half the days you're supposed to spend with him. The fact that you haven't called him once except on Friday nights to let him know when you'll pick him up. Should I go on?"

Hal remained stonily silent.

"You don't want a son," she said in a low voice. "You want a weapon to hold over my head, and I can assure you, Hal, that I will never, ever allow you to use Brian that way. He's a great kid and he still loves you. Don't do anything to cost yourself that love."

Hal sighed and sank down on the sofa. He ran his hand through his thinning hair. "All this stuff you get yourself mixed up in, it makes me crazy. What's happened to you?"

Molly regarded him sadly. "I've grown up."

"You consider it grown-up to get yourself involved in two murder investigations within six months?"

"Dammit, Hal, I don't go out searching for dead bodies. But when something like these murders happens, I'm going to do whatever I can to see that the killer is caught."

"That's why we have police, or hadn't you heard? Maybe that's the real truth. You've got the hots for that Cuban cop who was hanging around here on Sunday."

"Whether I do or don't is none of your concern. Now, if you don't mind, I need to spend a few minutes with Brian before I go back to work. You can let yourself out."

With that she left him where he was sitting and went to Brian's room. She found him staring at a video game on the TV screen. Some kind of ooze was swallowing up the good guys and her son was doing nothing to stop it. She sat down beside him.

"You okay?"

"I guess." He looked at her solemnly. "He wanted me to go home with him. I told him I couldn't, not without asking you." Tears welled up in his eyes. "I don't have to go, do I?"

"Of course you don't have to go. Not today. But your father does love you. Sometimes he just doesn't see how to let you know that. Can you try to remember that and give him a chance?"

"I love him, too, but not when he acts all crazy the way he did today."

"He did that because he was worried about you and mad at me."

"Why?"

"He thinks because Greg Kinsey was killed that you might be in danger too."

"That's dumb."

"I know that and you know that, but your dad worries. Remember how you used to be scared of the dark until he showed you that there was nothing hiding in the closets or under the bed? We need to show him that the things he's scared about aren't there either. Okay? Can you help me do that?''

He swiped his tears away with the back of his hand. "Has he gone?"

"I think so."

"Can I go to Kevin's now?"

She ruffled his hair, which was about as much affection as he would allow these days without squirming. "You bet," she told him. "I'll try to get home early. We'll order a pizza."

"Neato," he said, his grin back in place. "See you, Mom."

"Yeah, see you." *I love you,* she said to herself.

• • •

A half hour later Molly stood outside Jenkins's office and tried to work up the courage to knock on the door. Not only did Michael look busy, he looked angry. Either the papers in front of him didn't contain the information he'd hoped for or it was worse than he'd expected. She figured it was a toss-up as to which it was. The only way to find out was to go inside.

She opened the door and stepped into the cramped room. "Should I go or stay?" she asked when he finally looked up.

"Stay," he said grimly. He waved in the general direction of a chair buried under layers of files.

"Wasn't the report what you'd hoped it would be?"

"It's interesting," he said, tossing it over. "Take a look."

Surprised, Molly took the faxes and began to

read through them. They were the investigator's reports on Jeffrey Meyerson. While they didn't offer anything concrete to prove that he hadn't sneaked into town, shot Kinsey, and then feigned a much later arrival, they also shot the hell out of the theory that he'd latched on to Veronica for her money.

Jeffrey Meyerson owned enough property in Beverly Hills, Santa Monica, and Malibu to support a hundred households in lavish style. He'd inherited some, parlayed his investments into a level of wealth that few men even imagined, and shared his bounty with half the charities in Los Angeles. He had an apartment in Rome, another in Paris, one in London, and an entire floor in a co-op facing Central Park in New York.

According to half a dozen bankers, real estate experts, and civic leaders, the only tarnish on Meyerson's glittering record was a brief bout with an addiction to pain-killers prescribed following a particularly nasty bumpy landing of his private plane. He'd considered that a warning and had sold the jet thereafter and booked himself into first class on commercial flights. His most recent had been on Saturday night into Miami.

He had never dabbled in Hollywood's riskiest business, films, until this past year when he'd taken a gamble on a small studio that reportedly insisted on a high level of artistic integrity.

Molly glanced up. "Let me guess. That studio was financing this picture for GK Productions."

"Bingo."

"Is that how Veronica got the part?"

"Les says everyone at the studio is very tight-lipped about which came first, the financing or Greg's casting of Veronica."

"It would devastate her to discover that he only hired her to please Jeffrey."

"And we don't know that's what happened. Care to make a few calls to your contacts and see what the scuttlebutt is?" he asked.

"Vince won't like it."

"Blame it on me. Besides, he'll like it even less if we don't solve this case in the next day or two."

Molly tried to determine who might know more about how the financing for *Endless Tomorrows* was arranged. Laura Crain would doubtlessly know. So would Daniel Ortiz. Unfortunately, they were both on hand and still considered suspects. She doubted they'd want to chat about Meyerson's role in GK Productions.

Unofficially, though, one person in L.A. might talk. Greg's agent, the man who'd put the deal together. Alan Nivens had the hottest agency in town at the moment. He liked to boast of the deals he made, and Greg had been one of his most shining success stories. Molly had met him once on a trip to the Coast and knew he had been influential in convincing Greg to film in Miami.

She flipped open the thick address book she kept in her purse and dialed his number. His secretary put her right through.

"Alan, I'm so sorry about what happened to Greg," she said.

"I know you are, babe. I'm devastated. Everyone

out here's in mourning. Do the cops know any more?"

"They're working on it. You could help them out, though."

"Anything, babe. Name it. I won't rest until I know Greg's killer is in jail."

"What do you know about a man named Jeffrey Meyerson?"

"Social bigwig, charities, real estate," he said without an instant's hesitation. Then more cautiously, he asked, "How'd his name crop up?"

"I hear he bankrolled this picture."

Now Alan did pause. "Where'd you hear it?"

"It doesn't matter. Is it true?"

"He put some money in it, yes."

"Before or after Greg cast Veronica Weston?"

Alan chuckled. "I knew I liked you, babe. You are one very smart cookie."

"Come on, Alan. Quit the flattery and tell me."

"Meyerson and Weston are an item. Everyone out here knows that."

"Is that why Greg cast her?" she repeated.

She heard Alan's fingers drumming on his desk.

"Absolutely not," he said finally, a little too emphatically. "He liked her work, or at least that's what he told me. I couldn't shake him on it. Meyerson got into the act later. Much later, as a matter of fact. Greg didn't want to go to him at all, but Veronica insisted when she realized the picture might not get made."

"Thanks," she said. "I'll keep you posted on the investigation."

"They gonna release Greg's body soon? We want to schedule a memorial."

"I'm sure his family will be contacted as soon as the police say it's okay."

"He has no family. They should call me. The kid was like a son to me. I'll take care of the arrangements."

Since Alan Nivens wasn't much more than ten years older than Greg, Molly doubted the sentiment, but she didn't call him on it. "I'll see that the police are told," she said.

"Told what?" Michael wanted to know as soon as she'd hung up.

"That Alan wants to be notified when Greg's body can be released. He wants to schedule a memorial service."

"Should be in a day or two. What else did he have to say? I gathered from what you said he knew about Meyerson's involvement with the film."

"He swears the appeal to Meyerson was a last-ditch attempt to salvage the film. Veronica insisted on asking him, reportedly against Greg's wishes. No one else wanted to play, probably because of Veronica's reputation for drinking, although Alan didn't come out and say that."

"So Jeffrey didn't demand the casting as part of his agreement to finance?"

"Alan swears hiring Veronica was Greg's decision and that it came prior to the contact with Meyerson. He doesn't know why Greg insisted on it so stubbornly."

While they both tried to figure out the implica-

tions of the report and what Molly had learned earlier from Duke, the phone rang. As Michael listened
to the caller, only a slight widening of his eyes gave
any indication that he found what was being said to
be fascinating.

"Well?" Molly demanded the minute he'd hung
up.

"Just wait."

"For what?"

Before he could respond, the fax began spewing
out pages. Michael picked them up and started to
read. His blank expression didn't give away anything. It was driving Molly nuts.

"Are you going to share or am I going to have
to rip those pages away from you?"

Michael stared at the report for another full
minute before tossing it over to Molly. "See what
you make of this."

"What?"

"Just read it."

The investigator had faxed a report from a private hospital about a hundred miles north of Los
Angeles. It was dated slightly more than thirty-one
years earlier. The name on the top meant nothing
to her.

"Who on earth is Francine Weatherly?"

"According to Les's sources in L.A., that was the
name of a character from a movie."

"A movie? When?"

"Thirty, thirty-one years ago. The role was
played by Veronica Weston. It earned her an Academy Award nomination for best supporting actress."

Molly gaped. "You're suggesting that Veronica

entered some hospital using her character's name as a pseudonym nearly thirty-one years ago? Why bother? She certainly didn't hide the fact that she went into that alcohol treatment program last year."

"Maybe she felt that was a whole lot more socially acceptable than having a child out of wedlock and giving the baby away."

Molly regarded him with astonishment. "She had a baby? That's never been reported. Never."

"Obviously that was the point."

Molly didn't believe it. Beyond the bouts of drinking, there had never been the slightest hint of scandal surrounding Veronica Weston. Granted, she didn't strike Molly as the maternal type, but would she have given up a baby for adoption and kept the secret all these years? She studied the hospital record and the attached birth certificate trying to imagine some other conclusion. She couldn't come up with one.

"There's something more, isn't there?" she said, studying Michael's disgustingly smug expression. She'd seen that expression on his face before, always when he was this close to wrapping up a case.

"Haven't you figured it out yet?" he said with an infuriating, teasing glint in his eyes.

"Stop playing guessing games with me and spit it out."

"Look at the birthdate," he urged patiently. "Look familiar?"

June 15, 1961. It was familiar because the cast had celebrated a birthday on that date. Greg Kinsey's birthday.

"Oh, dear God," Molly murmured as she finally made the connection. "You're suggesting that Veronica was Gregory's mother, aren't you?" She stared at Michael. "Is that really possible? Are you sure?"

"I'm not sure of anything, but it would certainly explain why Gregory was so determined to give her a break. It would explain those vibes Duke said he felt whenever he was around the two of them."

"You think Greg knew she was his mother?"

"It's the only thing that makes sense. Les is still checking out whether he could have found out. I expect another call in a few minutes. He has some sources with those groups that help adoptees track down their natural parents. Besides, I'm not that fond of coincidences, at least not whoppers like this."

"What about Veronica, though? Does she know?"

"That's the big question, isn't it? What do you think?"

"I don't think so." She hesitated. "On the other hand, maybe that would explain some of the tension between the two of them. If she was feeling guilty, she'd probably be very short-tempered."

She stared at Michael, her eyes stinging with tears at the implication. "My God, can you imagine what she must be going through, if she does know? How could anyone hide that kind of grief?" She shook her head. "She can't know. As much as I respect her acting abilities, I don't think even she is talented enough to cover up all the sorrow and guilt a mother would feel at the death of a son, especially a son she'd never acknowledged.''

Michael stood up. "There's only one way to find out. As soon as Les calls back, we'll go talk to Veronica.''

CHAPTER
SIXTEEN

Molly checked the production schedule and saw that shooting was to end by dusk. It was nearly eight thirty now. In no more than an hour Veronica would be back at the hotel having dinner and studying her lines for the next day.

The film's already rigorous shooting schedule had become even tighter with the necessity of making up for the delays due to Greg's death and earlier snafus in production. Violent thunderstorms had postponed one day of outdoor shots. Another day had stalled when three key people had gotten food poisoning from food left too long without refrigeration on location.

"I think we should wait and go to the hotel," she told Michael. "Veronica shouldn't hear something like this on location, not with everyone around."

"You're right. Let's grab a sandwich or something and then get over to the hotel to wait."

"Just let me call Brian. I promised him pizza tonight."

Michael regarded her evenly. "Maybe that's not a promise you should break." Years of childhood separation from his own mother had made him ultra sensitive to parent-child relationships.

Molly was torn herself. Michael was right, especially after what had happened earlier with Hal. But Veronica was likely to need her, too. Least important but certainly a factor was her own curiosity.

If what Michael was surmising about the relationship between Greg and Veronica was true, then everything hinged on whether the actress knew about it. If she hadn't known, then she could still reasonably be considered a strong suspect. If she had known—or even guessed without actual confirmation—then Molly couldn't believe that Veronica could have fired the shot that killed her son.

"If Liza's home, maybe she'll order pizza tonight. Then I'll make it up to Brian tomorrow."

"I thought you left Liza on location with Duke Lane."

"I did, but he promised to drive her home. I think he wrapped up earlier today than Veronica. It only takes about five minutes to get to the condo from Virginia Key."

Liza picked up on the second ring. She was at home with Duke Lane. Molly knew better than to think it was anything more than mutual love of the environment, so she didn't hesitate to ask if Brian could join them.

"I think there's been a break in the case. I'd like to stay here and see how it plays out."

"What's happened?" Liza asked.

"I can't say yet. Not until we know more."

"We?"

"The police," Molly corrected over the sound of Liza's disbelieving laughter. She added defensively, "I'm involved, too, you know."

"You're nosy," Liza countered. "So am I. Stop in the minute you get home. Brian will be fine here with us. Should I call down to Kevin's or will you?"

"I'll call. I need to explain to him why I'm breaking a promise."

Brian took the news with stoic good humor. "You always want squishy mushrooms on the pizza, anyway. Liza doesn't like those."

Molly teased him right back. "Liza also won't let you eat meat, kiddo, so forget the sausage and pepperoni."

"Who says? She always lets me order anything I want. She just picks it off of her part and I get extra."

"Sounds like a deal to me."

"You gonna catch the killer tonight?"

"I don't know," Molly said honestly. "But we may be getting close to figuring it out."

"Is Michael with you?" he asked, a worried note creeping into his voice.

"Yes."

She heard his tiny sigh of satisfaction. "Then he'll take care of you."

Molly glanced across the desk and met Michael's gaze. "You bet," she said.

"Can I talk to him?"

"Sure." She handed the phone across the desk, then listened to Michael's solemn conversation with her son.

"I promise," he vowed, his gaze still holding hers. "I will take very good care of your mother. Later, sport."

When he'd hung up, a smile played about his lips. "I guess I have my job cut out for me."

"Oh?" she said, her cheeks flaming. There was no telling what instructions Brian had given on her behalf.

"I am not to keep you out too late. I am not to let you get anywhere near a gun. And I am not to let you get kidnapped by the killer again." He smiled ruefully. "He reminded me that I fell down on the job last time."

"He still thinks you walk on water."

"And you?"

"I think I'll plead the Fifth on that one."

"Worried about incriminating yourself, huh?"

"Never mind. Can we get out of here now? I feel Otis Jenkins's hostility practically bouncing off these walls."

"I know what you mean. Fortunately, I talked the brass into letting him be the one to fly out to L.A. to dig around for things like the incorporation papers on GK Productions and Greg's will. He was more than happy to be out of this head-to-head rivalry. He should be there soon. Hopefully, he can dig up something concrete by tomorrow. Les said he'd help him with contacts."

They were nearly out the door when Francesca

and her photographer came up the steps of the police station.

"What brings you two over this way?" Michael inquired. "Not thinking of flying back to Italy, are you?"

"We would like to go, yes," Giovanni replied. "Can you not release us, if we promise to fly back any time we are needed?"

Michael shook his head. "Sorry. I just need you to stick around a few days more." He still held their passports to assure their compliance.

Francesca muttered a torrent of Italian. The photographer retorted with one terse word, which silenced her for a moment. She appealed to Molly with a look. "I wish to say good-bye to Gregory. Is possible?"

Molly gaped at her. "You want to go to the morgue?"

Giovanni threw up his hands in a gesture of frustration. "She is crazy. I cannot talk her out of this. She says she needs, how can I say in English, to closing the door."

Even with the slight mangling of the phrase, Molly understood what he meant. Naturally the young girl felt she needed closure, but Molly shook her head. "I don't think this would be a good idea," she told her. "His wound is very bad. You would not like to remember him like this."

Michael put a hand on the model's shoulder. "She's right. Let it go."

Francesca uttered a tremulous sigh, her expression defeated. "I cannot do this?"

"You could," Michael said gently. "But I would advise against it."

She looked from him to Molly, then to Giovanni. "I will not go, then."

The photographer put his arm around her and led her away.

"She's not really on your list of suspects anymore, is she?"

"The long list, not the short list," Michael replied, watching the girl leave. "That photographer could make the short list, though. He's obsessed with her."

"That's what I thought, too. And he admits coming to Veronica's trailer after her."

"Where would he get a gun, though? It always comes back to that. He didn't bring one into the country. I checked on that."

"This is Miami," she reminded him. "Guns aren't exactly impossible to lay your hands on."

"If you know where to look, who to ask. You think he knows the right people?"

"Probably not," she admitted. "But neither does Veronica."

"We'll see," he said. "We'll see."

• • •

An hour later, after they'd sampled several appetizers at an upscale Middle Eastern restaurant, Molly and Michael took the elevator up to Veronica's suite. Jeffrey Meyerson greeted them at the door, his expression unwelcoming.

"We need to have a talk with Ms. Weston," Michael told him.

"Now's not a good time," Jeffrey said. "Couldn't you come back later? Maybe tomorrow."

"No," Michael said. "We need to see her now."

"It's okay, darling," Veronica called from the bedroom. "Let them in."

Jeffrey looked unhappy, but he stepped out of their way and gestured toward the living room. A room service tray held coffee, cups, and half-eaten chicken salad sandwiches on croissants. A pale pink rosebud—a lover's gesture or a hotel nicety—provided a festive note to the skimpy meal. An empty vodka bottle had been upended in the trash can and a fresh bottle, its cap still off, sat on the wet bar. Obviously Veronica had given up any pretense of being on the wagon.

Jeffrey rinsed out the cups, dried them, and offered coffee. His hand shook as he poured the still-steaming liquid into two cups. Either he was hung over from the luncheon champagne he'd finished off or very nervous. Molly wondered again what Jeffrey Myerson had to be nervous about. His gaze kept darting to the manila folder Michael had placed on the credenza.

It was fifteen minutes before Veronica joined them. During that time Jeffrey kept up a constant barrage of inconsequential chatter, like a host making small talk with strangers at a dinner party arranged by his wife for her friends.

Veronica swept into the room at last, her trademark chiffon billowing behind, this time in a shade of pale yellow that erupted into brilliant orange at the hem.

"I'm so sorry to have kept you waiting," she

said as she waved in the general direction of the bottle of vodka. Jeffrey took the hint and poured a double shot over ice. He handed the heavy crystal glass to her and served up a warning look at the same time.

"What can I do for you?" Veronica asked. Nothing in her tone or her manner betrayed any hint of nervousness.

"I'd like you to take a look at this, see if it means anything to you," Michael said, handing her the folder. Jeffrey looked as if he wanted to snatch it away from her.

Veronica took one look at the hospital record and birth certificate made out in the name of Francine Weatherly and turned the shade of library paste. She crumpled into an armchair, the swirls of chiffon settling around her.

"Are you okay?" Molly asked, concerned by her lack of color.

"No," Veronica said flatly. She stared at Michael. "What does this have to do with anything? Why would you dredge up something like this after all these years? It can't possibly have any bearing on the case."

Before Michael could respond, Molly stepped in. She sat beside Veronica and held the woman's hand as she said gently, "Look at the birth certificate again, the date. Remember when we celebrated Greg's birthday?"

"What are you saying?" Veronica whispered, her eyes wide with shock.

"I'm asking you if there is any chance, any

chance at all, that Gregory could have been your son.''

"Oh, my God," Veronica said, tears spilling down her cheeks. "Oh, my God."

Jeffrey looked as if he wanted to murder the pair of them. "Why did you have to blurt it out like that? Leave us alone," he demanded. "Just leave us alone."

Michael regarded him apologetically. "I'm afraid we can't do that. If it's true, this could have a material bearing on this case." He turned a compassionate gaze on Veronica. "Is there any chance?"

Her hands covering her face, Veronica nodded. "It's possible, but I didn't know. I swear to you I didn't know."

"We think that Greg did know."

"He did," Jeffrey said, defeat in his voice. "I spoke to him on the day he died. I had always thought there was something a little odd about the way he fought so hard to keep Veronica on this film. At first I thought it was simply that he liked her work, wanted to give her a chance to redeem herself, but as time went on, I saw that it was much more than that. I did a little investigating of my own."

Veronica regarded him incredulously. "You knew? You knew and you never said a word to me? How could you, Jeff? How could you do that to me?"

"I had to, my dear. Can't you see that? I didn't want to tell you until I knew for certain. When I found out, I asked Greg about it. He admitted it. We both agreed that I should be here when he told you.

That's why I flew in on Saturday, to be with you when you found out that he was your son. When I got here and discovered that he'd been murdered, I didn't know what to do. I wasn't sure what the implications were."

"So you never said a word to anyone?" Molly asked.

"Not one word," he confirmed.

"Did anyone else know?"

"To my knowledge, no."

"But someone must have," Molly said. "Someone who would have benefited from Greg's will, but only if he had no living relatives."

"Exactly," Michael concurred. "I hope to hell Jenkins can get his hands on that will tonight."

Molly's gaze was fixed on Veronica. She looked shattered, as if nothing in the world made sense to her anymore. Molly guessed she needed to talk, to say out loud what she had hidden for all these years.

"It just can't be," she said over and over. "It would be too bizarre, too awful."

Michael said, "It's probably not necessary now that we know he admitted the truth to Jeffrey, but I'm trying to get Gregory's adoption records unsealed. What I have so far indicates that he was adopted by a wealthy Santa Barbara family. The birth date matches."

Veronica kept shaking her head. "I never knew," she said sorrowfully. "I never understood why he wanted so much to work with me, why he fought the studio. You think it was because he knew even then, months ago?"

"Friends of his adoptive parents told police in

Santa Barbara that he'd been looking for his natural mother for several years. They said he knew it upset his parents, so he'd never told them whether he'd traced her. They both died not knowing if he'd succeeded.''

"Why did you give him up?" Molly asked, hoping that she was doing the right thing in trying to get the actress to open up. "In the sixties no one would have condemned you for having a child without being married."

Veronica shook her head. "You're wrong about that. My son wasn't illegitimate. I was married when he was conceived, but my husband was a real bastard. I didn't want him near my child."

Molly was shocked. "There's never been any mention of a marriage in any of the bios I've read, not back then."

"The studio kept it hushed up. I was barely eighteen when we got married and just getting a reputation as some sort of sex goddess. The studio and my husband, who'd directed my first two films, agreed it would spoil the image if the marriage were made public. Everyone was very paternalistic about it, and I was too naïve to argue."

"Then what happened?" Molly prodded, when Veronica seemed uninclined to go on. "Why did you give up your baby?"

Veronica took a deep breath. She kept her gaze fastened on Molly as if she couldn't bear to face anyone else in the room.

"When things fell apart, I tried to get a divorce, but by then my husband was convinced his fate was linked to mine. It was hard enough battling that without telling him about a baby. He would never have let me go.''

"But he did let you go,'' Molly said.

"In a way. I told everyone I needed to get away, to get my head together. Then I went into hiding for the last few months of the pregnancy. I arranged for a private adoption so there would be fewer official questions. I couldn't risk anything leaking out in the press. It was best all the way around to give up my son, but I never forgot about him. Never. I regretted it more than I can say, but it was the only way I could think of for both of us to survive.''

Again tears welled in her eyes. "Do you know the real tragedy of all this? I saw that Greg cared for me. Underneath all the fighting, all the screaming over the script, I could see that he really cared what happened to me on-screen. I didn't understand why it mattered so much to him, but it was there, always. The caring. The demand for every shot to be perfect. I thought it was simply that he was a perfectionist. He knew I was his mother and he loved me, but he never knew, *never*, how much I really loved the son I gave away.''

As Veronica wept over the loss of that son, over the harsh words they'd exchanged in the brief time they'd had together, Molly and Michael slipped out of the suite. In the elevator, Molly saw the haunting pain shadowing Michael's eyes and realized that memories of his own childhood must have been stirred by Greg and Veronica's tragedy. The years he had been alone in the U.S., his mother still in Cuba.

She silently slid her hand into his. At first he resisted. She could feel his muscles tense. Then he relaxed and curled his fingers around hers. He said nothing as they walked away from the hotel. He didn't need to. Even without words, she had never felt closer to him.

CHAPTER
SEVENTEEN

"I still can't figure out how we're any better off now than we were before we found out about the connection between Veronica and Gregory," Molly grumbled, trying to speak loudly enough to be heard over the sidewalk café's reggae band. "Knowing about the relationship, it would make more sense if he'd been furious over her abandonment and had killed her."

"Think about motive," Michael said patiently as his gaze automatically scanned the crowd. "Who has the best motive?"

Watching him, Molly wondered if he ever fully relaxed or if his cop instincts were always at work. She had a hunch that if she asked an hour from now he would be able to describe to the last detail what the patrons around them looked like, their mannerisms, and any visible idiosyncrasies they had.

"Are you listening to me?" he asked, when she'd gone a full five minutes saying nothing.

"Hmm?" Molly blinked, then wondered exactly why it was that they were possibly the only two people sitting here on a moonlit night with something other than romance on their minds. Maybe because murder had a dampening effect on the libido. She dragged her thoughts back to the gist of his question.

"I'm listening," she said.

"Okay, then. Would the relationship between the star and the director have given someone else a motive to kill him?"

Michael sounded like an instructor trying to make a point to a rather dull, dim-witted student. Oddly enough, she didn't resent it. At least he was sharing information with her, treating her insights with respect, forcing her to be analytical rather than emotional. Personally, she thought a good blend of gut instinct and a keen eye for the facts were exactly what made him such a good detective. He, however, seemed unwilling to admit to the conclusions he reached intuitively. She slowly sipped her wine and gave the question the consideration he obviously expected.

"Yesterday, before we found out about his background, I would have said Jeff Meyerson," she admitted. "He's engaged to Veronica. Or so he says. She doesn't seem all that committed. At any rate, if he's planning to marry her, maybe he didn't want a son in line as an heir to her estate. I should have known it would be too tidy and too obvious."

"Don't beat yourself up over it. You had the

right idea, just the wrong person, at least on that basis. From everything you told me, Veronica doesn't have much of an estate. She needed this job just to survive, right?''

"Yes. She told me as much."

"And he has a fortune."

"So we discovered. Then we can scratch Meyerson off the list?"

Michael shook his head. "Not so fast. What if he thought Greg was likely to ruin his relationship with Veronica, that she'd become so caught up in her newfound son that she would no longer spare any time for him? If he's obsessed with her, that could drive him to murder the competition."

Molly was shaking her head before he'd finished. "No way. If he truly loves her, he'd never rob her of the chance to know her son."

"I mentioned obsession, not love."

"If you're going for that angle, then I like our Italian photographer better. He's obsessed with the gorgeous, nubile Francesca."

"You just don't want it to be anyone you know."

"Maybe," she conceded. "It's no fun considering the possibility that someone you know is capable of pulling a gun and shooting down a friend, or at least someone who probably considered him or her a friend."

"Who's your choice, then? You know all of the players better than I do. Hank Murdock benefits from Kinsey's death because he'll get a shot at finishing the movie. Spice that with a professional rivalry and you have a decent motive."

"But he was in the production trailer with witnesses."

"All right, then, Duke Lane. What's his stake in this?"

"None I can imagine. Laura Crain might have pressured Greg into hiring Duke in the first place because of his box-office status, but he and Greg got along. He doesn't need all the publicity the murder has generated. Every female in America already knows who he is. Besides, from what I hear, he wants this picture wrapped in a hurry so he can get on with the next one. I wouldn't have given the man a lot of credit for brains a few days ago, but since then we've talked a couple of times. He's smart. He has to know that a murder at the least will delay production." She shook her head. "I think we can eliminate Duke."

"Too bad," Michael grumbled.

Molly grinned. "You just hate having a suspect who gets more press attention than you do."

He regarded her indignantly. "You're treading on thin ice, sweetheart. I can get you back on that suspect list faster than you can say 'Lights, camera, action.' "

Molly shook her head confidently. "I don't think so. You want to be out of Miami Beach and back on your own turf too badly to waste time trying to make a case against me."

"Maybe so," he said, sliding his sunglasses down a fraction to level a look at her. "But Otis Jenkins is just itching to take you on."

Molly decided this would be an excellent time

to divert Michael's attention in another direction. "How about Daniel Ortiz?"

"If he gets a bigger stake in GK Productions, maybe. Besides, witnesses place him on the set at the time of the shooting. He was setting up for the next shot."

Playing devil's advocate, Molly countered with, "He could have slipped away. Things are so chaotic between scenes, no one would have noticed if he'd left for a minute or two. Face it, that's all it would have taken to slip over to Veronica's trailer, wait for her to leave, then shoot Greg and count on Veronica's being blamed."

"If that's the scenario, then it had to be someone who didn't know she was his mother. No one would expect a mother to be blamed for shooting her son. How about Laura Crain? What do you think of her as a suspect?"

"Opportunity? Probably. She claims she was back at the hotel, but no one else was there with her."

"No one saw her on the set either."

"Which doesn't mean she wasn't there," Molly argued. "Again, everyone who's actually working has a lot going on between takes. Maybe they'd notice a stranger, but not someone connected with the film, someone they're used to seeing around all the time."

Something was troubling her, but she couldn't quite put her finger on it. She tried to envision the way events that night had unfolded, at least as they knew them.

Greg and Veronica had been inside her trailer,

arguing over the script. Then, as she'd been leaving, Francesca had barged in, furious because Greg didn't want her to stay in America with him. Giovanni had come after her, and the two of them had left together, or so he had said. With all that happening and only a limited time period between their departures and the discovery of the body, surely one of them should have spotted the killer, even if they weren't aware of it. Especially if the gunman had stood outside the trailer and fired.

Good Lord, that was it! No one in his right mind would have stood on the sidewalk and fired a gun, not with off-duty policemen at each end of the block and other members of the cast and crew all too likely to come along at any second. Greg's killer had to have been inside. She tried to recall the angle of his body in relation to the door, but her memory failed her. She hadn't wanted to remember the way he had looked.

Her excitement began to fade. What difference did it make? They already knew that in all likelihood Greg had been killed by someone who knew him. Anyone in the cast or crew could have traced him to Veronica's trailer, waited for him to be alone, and then gone in on some pretext or another.

"What are you thinking?" Michael asked.

Molly's head was reeling and it wasn't from the wine. "How do you do this? From what I can see there are still a solid half-dozen people with either motive or opportunity."

"You just keep narrowing things down, until there's only one possible conclusion. Then you pray you can come up with enough solid physical evidence to cinch the case."

"Let's talk about the physical evidence a minute. Was there anything odd inside the trailer?"

"Odd in what way?"

"I'm not sure. It just occurs to me that anyone who tracked Greg down in Veronica's trailer, then went in to shoot him may have had some sort of cover story, maybe script notes he needed to see, checks he needed to sign. I don't know. Was there anything in that trailer that shouldn't have been there?"

"Nothing that seemed particularly odd or out of place to me, but let's go check it out. The trailer's been impounded and sealed. I have bags of evidence at the station. Take your pick."

"The bags of evidence, I think."

"Let's go."

When Greg's personal effects were brought out, a shiver sped down Molly's spine. She felt as if she were invading his privacy as she looked through his wallet, then sorted through the rental car keys, some loose change, and a dozen or so scraps of paper. Most of them were little pink message slips with names written in Laura's careful, schoolgirl printing. A couple were scrawled by a masculine hand. Probably Jerry's.

Molly studied the slips. She recognized most of the callers. Alan Nivens had placed three separate calls that night. Jeffrey Meyerson had called once, much earlier in the day. A reporter for *Variety* had called wanting to confirm a rumor. The message didn't note what the rumor was, but apparently

Greg had guessed. He had crumpled that message into a tiny ball. Francesca had called twice. And several men whom Molly knew to be connected with the studio had called within minutes of each other.

Those last messages were written in a cramped, angry script. Apparently Laura had been furious about something, perhaps at them, perhaps at having just been forced to convey a message from her competition for Greg's affections. Her pencil had actually poked a hole in the paper on one of the messages.

"Look at this," she said, handing Michael the messages. "Look at the way Laura was bearing down. There's a hole. She must have been irate."

"Over what, though?"

"Being pestered by Francesca and taking it out on the calls that followed?"

"Why didn't she just ignore Francesca's calls, not tell him about them at all? She wrote those messages in a nice, precise hand."

"It would go against the grain for a woman like Laura to fail in her duties, though I'm sure she was tempted to do just that. Besides, Francesca would probably ask Greg why he hadn't returned her calls. He'd guess what had happened and Laura couldn't risk that. She certainly didn't want him to fire her."

Suddenly Molly recalled the way Laura had looked when she'd finally walked into the production trailer after Greg's body had been found. She'd looked tearful, but controlled. Not grief stricken. Molly remembered thinking at the time that it was quite a performance for a woman whose lover had just been shot.

She glanced over the messages again and noted the times they were taken. The last call from Francesca had come barely an hour before she and Jerry had found Greg's body. The calls from the studio came in right after that.

"I think maybe we need to have a talk with Laura," Molly said.

"About?"

"What exactly went on the last time she saw Greg. Judging from these messages, it had to have been in that time span between the time Veronica left Greg in her trailer and the time he was killed."

Michael took the messages back and studied them. "The time's on here, but not the date. He could have been carrying these around for days."

Molly shook her head. "Greg was methodical about messages, in part because of the time difference between here and L.A. He made it a point to go back to pick up his messages about eight every night. That meant it was only five on the Coast and he could return any calls before people left for the day."

"This was Saturday. Would he have worried about business calls on the weekend?"

"Look at the messages. He was getting calls at all hours, every day. Every one of these messages came in between six o'clock and ten P.M."

"But what day?"

"It had to have been Saturday. Otherwise, he would have returned the calls and tossed the messages."

Michael nodded. "If you're sure of that, then let's go have a talk with Laura. If we can place her in that trailer at the critical time, we definitely have a liar."

"More important, we may have a killer." Considering the way she felt about Laura Crain, nothing would have pleased Molly more.

CHAPTER
EIGHTEEN

They were in the creaking hotel elevator on their way to the production office when Michael's beeper went off. When he saw the calling number, he promptly punched the button to take them straight back down to the first floor.

"Who is it?" Molly wanted to know. It had to be important to keep him from going after the probable killer.

"Jenkins. He could have found something. We ought to know that before we go in to see Laura."

"I could go ahead," Molly suggested, counting on the statistics that indicated a single crime of passion was not indicative of a penchant for shooting down everyone in sight. Maybe she could wrench an admission from Laura by giving her a shoulder to cry on.

"I don't think so," Michael said.

"But I could tell her I needed to check the production schedule. She'd never know what I was really there for. Maybe she'd open up, if I sounded sympathetic. She doesn't really have a woman around to talk to."

"I thought your impression was that she didn't much like women. Besides, exactly how much snooping around do you figure you could accomplish before she caught on?"

"I'm counting on you to arrive before we get to that point."

"And if I'm delayed?"

"I'll beat a hasty retreat. I promise."

"I need only ask your son about tonight to have a pretty good idea what your promises are worth."

Because the barb struck home, Molly glared at him. "Was that reminder entirely necessary?"

He nodded, his expression grim. "I thought so."

Since his impression of her was so low anyway, Molly didn't feel the least bit guilty for the last-second dash she made back into the elevator as the doors slid closed. She felt an instant's satisfaction as she caught Michael's stunned expression. Or maybe that had been fury.

Okay, so what she was doing was rash and impulsive and foolhardy. She wasn't actually going to accuse Laura of anything, though. She'd just snoop around a little, sound her out. Maybe she'd even stumble across a gun. Laura might not know Miami well enough to have taken the murder weapon and pitched it into some nearby body of water. There were plenty to choose from, of course, but maybe the producer hadn't been thinking clearly enough to dispose of the gun right away. Hell, it could have been in the bottom of that voluminous purse she carried with her everywhere.

To her surprise, the door to the production office was closed and locked. She knocked, but no one answered. All the better, she thought, as she used the key she'd been issued on the first day of production.

Inside, one lamp burned dimly, casting eerie shadows around the room. The heavy drapes had been drawn, blocking out the silvery moonlight that shimmered on the ocean and at least some of the noise from the street. Suddenly the room seemed spookier than she remembered, perhaps because she'd never been in it alone and at night before. Perhaps because its usual occupant might very well be a murderer.

She wondered if Michael would take the next elevator up after her or if she had time to do some genuine sleuthing. As much as she wanted to poke freely around in drawers, she was forced to admit that she wished he'd hurry up. The closed, dreary atmosphere was giving her the creeps.

So get busy, she told herself. She moved deliberately to the desk and began opening drawers. They were every bit as organized as Laura herself. Files were neatly labeled and in alphabetical order. Bills had been sorted and stamped according to date received. Payment check numbers had been noted. Payroll records were in their own orderly drawer. It all seemed a little compulsive, even to someone used to keeping her own files relatively organized.

Still, so far it was pretty boring stuff, Molly

noted as she came upon a file of contracts. Most were standard, according to what she knew of the industry. Duke got a hefty bonus at various stages of the film's success. Veronica's deal guaranteed her specific perks suitable to a legendary glamour queen. The cost was insignificant for most, but they underlined her status as being one step above everyone in the cast except Duke.

A quick scan of the remaining contracts revealed deals with everyone in the cast and crew with the exception of Hank, Daniel, and Laura herself. Molly guessed that was because all of them owned a piece of GK Productions and had their own separate salary arrangements because of it.

The bottom drawer in the desk was locked. Molly found a paper clip, bent it until it was nearly straight, then tried to jimmy the lock. As she was working at it, she noticed scratches in the surrounding wood. They had been there before she'd started her amateur attempt at lock picking. Someone else had wanted access to this very same drawer. Since the desk had been brought in especially for the production office, she knew with absolute certainty that those marks were recent. Presumably, though, Laura would have had a key. Who else would be interested in whatever was locked away?

To know that, she had to get inside. She knelt down to get a better view of the lock. She was still in that incriminating position when the connecting door to Laura's room swung open, filling the office with a bright stream of light.

"What the hell do you think you're doing?"

Laura demanded, closing the door carefully behind her before crossing the room.

Molly was reasonably good at thinking on her feet. Unfortunately she wasn't on her feet. She was on her knees with a paper clip stuck in a locked drawer. She considered lying through her teeth and saying she needed the production schedule, but she knew only too well it was posted quite visibly on the bulletin board beside the door.

Recalling that there had been no file marked PERMITS, she said, "I was hunting for the permits you'll need for tomorrow's shooting schedule. I wanted to be sure you had them all and that they were up-to-date, now that we're running behind by a couple of days."

Laura continued to look skeptical, but she came over, nudged Molly aside and retrieved a file from the top of the desk, the one place Molly hadn't searched. She'd saved the obvious for last, figuring nothing incriminating would be in plain sight.

She stood up and took the file. "Thanks."

"It's awfully late," Laura noted, with a deliberate glance at her watch.

"I know, but I just thought of this and I wanted to be sure it was taken care of."

"You came all the way back from Key Biscayne? Why didn't you just call?"

"Actually, I was still in the neighborhood. I had a meeting with Veronica and it ran late. I stopped for a glass of wine after that."

"With that cop friend of yours?"

Molly nodded.

"Where is he, then?"

"He was beeped. He needed to make a call."

"He could have made it from up here."

"True. I guess he just wanted to be sure it was billed properly since it was long distance."

"Police business, then?"

Molly shrugged. "I assume so." She studied Laura. "I'm surprised you weren't in here working. You usually burn the midnight oil."

"Actually I was exhausted. I thought I'd get a decent night's sleep for a change. I haven't slept well at all since Greg was killed."

"I can imagine," Molly said, wondering why the producer would say she'd gone to bed early, when she was obviously still dressed in her street clothes. Of course, they were slightly disheveled. Maybe she'd fallen asleep with them on.

Laura had carefully put herself between Molly and the desk. Her expression perfectly bland, she said, "If there's nothing else, I think I'll lock up as soon as you've gone. I want to get back to bed."

Just then the phone rang, startling them both. Laura made no move to pick it up.

"Aren't you going to answer it?"

"No, it's late. The desk will take a message."

"Right," Molly said and started for the door. She stopped and turned back. "One last thing," she said, careful to keep her voice casual. "On the night Greg died he had a message from a reporter that seemed to upset him. Any idea what that was all about?"

Laura shot her an uneasy look. "I don't know what you're talking about."

"But you did take the message, didn't you?"

"Yes, but I didn't cross-examine the man. Now if that's all," she said pointedly.

Defeated, Molly backed toward the door. "I'll see you in the morning," she said as she carefully shut the office door behind her.

In the corridor she lingered outside Laura's door, not the least bit certain why she was doing it. She heard the faint click of the connecting door shutting, then the muffled squeak of mattress springs. Nothing suspicious in that. Laura was doing exactly what she'd said she was going to do. She was going back to bed.

And then Molly heard, plain as day, Hank Murdock saying, "What took you so long? Who was in there?"

Molly couldn't hear Laura's reply, which didn't much matter since she knew the answer.

"What the devil did she want?" Hank said.

Laura's voice rose slightly. "She said she was looking for the permits for tomorrow's shoot," she said defensively.

Silence followed, then Hank's voice. There was a new, unfamiliar tension to it. "Did you believe her?"

"No, but there's nothing in there that would be worth anything to her. Let her play amateur sleuth if she wants to. For God's sakes, Hank, the sooner they arrest someone for Greg's murder, the better off we'll all be."

Hank muttered a curse, but then the bedsprings squeaked again. Molly got the distinct impression from the subsequent silence that Laura had found a way to ease his mind. She had also given her a whole new angle to consider. She could hardly wait to get downstairs and tell Michael that Hank Murdock had apparently taken up where Greg Kinsey had left off with Laura Crain.

Molly waited nearly ten anxious minutes for the elevator to come before finally deciding it was stuck on another floor. She headed for the stairwell, recalling that Francesca had taken these same steps down on the night of Greg's murder to avoid bumping into Molly or the police.

Molly was halfway down to the street level when she heard running footsteps on the stairs. This wasn't someone who was stealthily sneaking up on her. It was someone in a hurry. Of course, with the elevator not functioning, it could be anyone. She reassured herself that there was no reason for the cold chill that swept over her or the suddenly quickened pumping of her heart.

She hurried her own steps, but the person was clearly gaining on her. She could practically hear whoever it was hitting three steps to every one of her own. The sound reverberated off the walls. She had only one more floor to go when a hand closed over her shoulder, scant inches from her neck where her pulse skittered wildly. A scream began deep inside but choked in her throat.

"Just listen to me, Molly," Laura said in a low voice. "If you do exactly as I say, you'll be just fine. My car is half a block down, right at the end of the alley. We're going to get in it. Understand?"

Since Molly figured Laura's gun was probably aimed about level with her heart, she had no delusions about disagreeing with the producer's plan.

The only thing she could do was stall for time, then pray that the side street was still so crowded with passersby that Laura would be able to do nothing if she made a break for it.

"Why, Laura? Why did you kill Greg?"

"I didn't," she said so convincingly that Molly stopped in her tracks.

She whirled around to stare at the producer. "You didn't?" she repeated, unable to keep the astonishment and disbelief out of her voice.

"No, you little fool. But I know who did. I'm trying to save your neck. Now will you hurry up and move before we both get our heads blown off."

This was probably no time for indulging in idle curiosity, but Molly couldn't help herself. "If you didn't do it, who did?"

"Three guesses and the first two don't count."

Suddenly Molly realized that only one person could have sent Laura plunging down this staircase after her. "Hank?" she breathed softly. "When did you know?"

Just then a door somewhere above them opened. "Laura?" Hank called. The plaintive tone of his voice sent a chill down Molly's spine.

Laura motioned toward the door and this time Molly didn't hesitate before racing down the remaining steps. She hit the bar across the door at full force, but it didn't budge.

"What's wrong?" Laura demanded, her gaze directed up the stairwell.

"It's jammed or locked."

"It can't be locked. It's a fire exit. Hit it harder."

Molly threw her full weight against the door just as Hank rounded the final turn in the stairwell. The door burst open just as he aimed his gun at the pair of them.

"I think we'll all leave together," he said softly, gesturing for them to precede him.

Molly was certain her legs would never move again. She froze where she was at the sight of the gun aimed directly at her.

"Move it," Hank said, nudging her with the gun. The cold press of metal sent acid pitching in her stomach.

"Why, Hank?" she said quietly. "Why did you kill him?"

He didn't answer. The only indication she had that he'd even heard her was the increased pressure of that gun against her ribs. He urged them relentlessly down that dark alley. There were no windows looking out on the alley at ground level, so it was unlikely anyone would see them from inside the hotel. Nor were there any cans or bottles she or Laura could kick, creating enough noise to draw attention. Their only chance would come when they reached the street. She tried to concentrate all of her attention on planning for that.

Perspiration beaded on her forehead and the nape of her neck. It ran in icy rivulets down her spine. Hank's silence was the worst of it, worse even than the terrifying press of the gun. If he would just talk to her, she could better sense his mood, better guess the exact moment she ought to run for it. She glanced at Laura and saw that she looked more resigned and weary than terrified.

When had her instincts deserted her? Until to-night she would have bet her life that Hank Murdock was incapable of murder. Now there was every indication that he had killed not only once, but intended to again. What could have driven this quiet, dedicated man to murder?

If he was involved with Laura, would he have been so incensed by Greg's moves on her that he finally shot him in a jealous rage? But why wait until almost the end of the picture? Could the timing have been a last desperate attempt to gain recognition as a director by completing the film in Greg's stead? The motives raced through her mind like film on fast forward, leaving impressions but no conclusions. Obviously Laura possessed some incriminating piece of information that she hadn't shared with anyone else. Did it have to do with those messages?

"Did you hate Greg?" she asked. "I thought the two of you were best of friends."

"We were," he said softly, an unexpected catch in his voice.

Molly seized on that faint hint of emotion. "Then he must have done something to make you very angry that night. What did he do?"

They were almost to the street. She could hear the laughter of a passing couple, the grinding start of a motorcycle. But there was still no response from Hank. The barrel of the gun seemed to tremble against her back. Because he was losing his nerve? Because something she'd said had reminded him that the man who'd died was, in fact, his best friend?

"Did I ever tell you how often Greg spoke of

you when we were making plans for this production?" she said. "He respected your work. Maybe even more than you did, he said. He was anxious to see that you got the break you deserved."

"Bullshit," he said succinctly. "He was going to force me out."

"Force you out," Molly repeated slowly. "Could he do that?"

"Yes," Laura said with a sigh. "He had the power to do it. You might as well tell her everything, Hank."

"A few years ago I had some heavy gambling debts," he said, reminding Molly of his claim that he hadn't been in the poker game that night because he no longer gambled.

"Greg loaned me the money to pay them off with my share of the company as collateral."

"But why would he force you out now?"

It was Laura who answered. "The studio had been on him for weeks about cutting overhead. With the picture close to done, they wanted Hank off the payroll. They waved a deal for additional films under his nose if he could streamline the company. That reporter had gotten wind of the studio's offer. He called Greg."

"And me," Hank added. "The son of a bitch called me. That's how I heard about it. Not from Greg. From some stupid reporter."

"You confronted him and he confirmed it," Molly said.

She dared to turn her head to catch a glimpse of him. His face was an expressionless mask, but his eyes were filled with some dark agony. As if he'd guessed what she could read in his eyes, he looked away. At the same time, they reached the street.

Molly used the tiny fraction of a second while Hank's attention was diverted to wrench free from his grasp and run. She lurched, nearly stumbled, then raced toward Ocean Drive, where she knew there would be more people and safety.

At the corner she ran headlong into Michael. His arms came around her, steel bands of comfort and courage. His gaze locked on hers. "You're okay?"

"Yes," she said shakily. "Go or Hank will get away. Laura's car is at the end of the alley. She's still with him."

Instead, he pulled her tight against him, so she could feel the thundering beat of his heart. "So help me God, if you ever, ever do anything that stupid again, I will break every single bone in your body myself," he swore fervently, adding an empassioned speech in Spanish that she suspected was better left untranslated.

"I'm okay. I swear it. Please, go after Hank."

"He's not going anywhere. He's waiting with Laura right by his car."

Molly's head snapped up. She glanced down the block and saw Hank leaning against the front fender, his shoulders slumped. Laura was holding the gun as if it were something distasteful.

"He's giving up?" she said incredulously.

Michael nodded. "Looks that way," he said as two other officers went down the block to take Hank into custody. As they passed by on their way back to the police cruisers on Ocean Drive, Molly stopped Laura. "Thank you for coming after me."

"I didn't do it for you," Laura said bluntly. "I couldn't let Hank get in any more trouble than he's already in. It was partly my fault in the first place. If only I'd told him what I suspected, he might have been prepared. I might have been able to make him see that it was purely a business decision, that it had nothing to do with his worth as a director. Instead, when that reporter hit him with it, he felt betrayed, by Greg, by me. Add to that the rumors he had to contend with all the time about Greg and me . . ." She shrugged. "It's no wonder he snapped."

"But the gun," Molly said. "Where did he get the gun?"

"I had it. Since I had to deal with large amounts of money occasionally, I got it for protection. He knew where I kept it."

"But you didn't know he'd taken it?"

"No. Not until tonight when everything started to add up." She glanced at Michael. "You knew, didn't you?"

At Michael's nod, Molly regarded them both with surprise. "When?" she said to Michael.

"Otis Jenkins had a talk with the studio. They told him about cutting Hank loose. He also found out that Laura had a permit for the gun. I tried to call you in the suite twice to warn you to be careful if he was around."

"I only heard the phone ring once," Molly said.

"Hank took the second call," Laura said. "I heard enough to guess what was happening. That's when I came after you."

"Thank you again."

"Can I go to the police station with Hank?" Laura asked Michael.

"No, but I'll give you a lift over there. I have to get over to headquarters and wrap this up. Just give me a couple of minutes with Molly."

Laura nodded and walked away.

"Can you get home okay?" he said, his fingers splayed against her cheek.

"Sure," she said. She'd finally stopped shaking at least five minutes back. "There's one more thing I don't understand."

"What's that?"

"On the night Jeffrey pushed Veronica, was there really a shot?"

"Yes. Hank thought she'd seen him coming out of Greg's trailer that night."

"But when the first shot missed, he never tried to kill her again."

"Probably because he knew by then that Veronica hadn't seen him."

"I wonder how she's doing?"

"Why don't you go up and see her? She'd probably be glad to have a friend around, now that her son's killer has been caught."

Molly touched his cheek. "That's what I love about you. For a tough cop, you're a real softie."

He grinned. "Don't let it get around. It'll ruin me on the streets."

She had started into the hotel, when he said, "Molly."

She turned back.

"I'll give you a call about Sunday."

When Molly regarded him blankly, he said, "The dinner at Tio Pedro's. You aren't going to chicken out on me, are you?"

"Not a chance," she said bravely. After tonight meeting Michael's family would have to be a piece of cake.

Be sure to catch Sherryl Woods's
next exciting mystery,

HOT MONEY

coming soon from Dell.

CHAPTER
ONE

As Molly DeWitt listened to two elegantly clad women scheme to take a Miami philanthropist to the monetary cleaners, she tried to recall exactly how her neighbor and best friend, Liza Hastings, had managed to talk her into showing up for this black tie charity affair. The last thing she remembered clearly was saying an emphatic *no*.

That had been a month ago. The next day the fancy, embossed invitation had appeared in her mailbox. A week after that, Liza had begun dropping pointed hints about her failure to reply, especially when the cause was so worthwhile—saving the spotted owls in Washington among other endangered creatures.

"I replied. I said *no*," Molly recalled saying quite clearly.

The ensuing discussion about the responsibilities of friendship had lasted no more than one or two weighty moments. Then Liza had left her to wage a battle with her conscience.

It wasn't that Molly had no conscience. It was simply that she'd grown up attending lavish affairs like this and had sworn on the date of her debut that she never would again. It had always seemed to her that if the women in the room had donated an amount equivalent to the cost of their gowns, there would have been no need for a fund-raiser at all. She could recall mentioning that to Liza on a number of occasions. Liza, unfortunately, had very selective hearing and a skill at arm-twisting unrivaled on the professional wrestling circuit.

The clincher, of course, had been Liza's persuasive appeal to Michael O'Hara. For a hard-nosed, macho homicide detective, the man had the resistance of mush when it came to saying no to a woman as committed to a cause as Liza was.

"What are we doing here?" he asked now as he nabbed another glass of champagne from a passing waiter.

Molly thought he sounded rather plaintive. She scowled at him. "We wouldn't be here if you hadn't succumbed to Liza's pressure. You had your checkbook out and those tickets in your hands before she even finished saying *please.*"

"You could have stopped me."

"How was I to know you intended to drag me along with you? For all I knew you planned to ask that charming go-go dancer who was all over you at Tio Pedro's a few weeks ago."

He grinned. "Go-go dancer? Your claws are

showing, Molly. Marielena is in the chorus of a Tony-Award-winning musical on Broadway."

"Whatever."

"Besides, I was hardly likely to ask her when this is your friend's event. I'm almost certain Liza indicated this was a package deal—you and the tickets, all for a paltry five hundred dollar contribution." He groaned. "Do you know how many tickets to Miami Heat games I could buy with that?"

"Don't tell me. Tell Liza. I'm wearing a dress that cost nearly double that."

"I thought a former debutante would have an entire collection of ball gowns."

"I do. In size four. I'm an eight now and if you make one single snide remark about how I could have starved myself back into those fours, I will personally dump the next tray of champagne I see over your head."

He regarded her curiously. "Are you always this charming at galas?"

Molly felt a momentary pang of guilt. She squashed it. "I get testy when I spend more than a week's pay on a dress that with any luck I will not wear again in this lifetime."

"At least you can save it for the Academy Awards or the Emmys, even the Miami Film Festival. Surely in your position with the film office sooner or later you'll have to drag it out again. Where is a cop supposed to wear a tux?"

"Save it for your wedding," she shot back. Considering Michael's avowed status as an eligible bachelor, it was as close to a curse as Molly could come. The alarm in his eyes improved her mood considerably. She linked her arm through his. "Toss down the last of that champagne and let's go mingle."

Actually, now that she was beginning to resign herself to an endless, tedious evening of polite chit-chat and lavish praise of the canapés, Molly discovered that she could appreciate the setting, if not the reason for her presence.

For the event Liza had commandeered Vizcaya, the closest thing Miami had to a palace. Built on a grand scale, the winter home of industrialist James Deering faced Biscayne Bay, which dutifully shimmered like a sea of diamonds under the full moon. A soft breeze, laced with the tang of salt air, swept over the estate. Most of the crowd was milling around under a striped refreshment tent on the south lawn or walking through the surrounding gardens.

The romantic setting was perfect for stealing kisses or seducing the high rollers into parting with their money. Molly caught sight of Liza amid a cluster of Miami's well-to-do socialites. They were all preening for the photographer from the morning paper. Liza's dramatic, offbeat dress in a shade referred to as tangerine—at least in the produce section, if not on the fashion pages—looked as out of place in the midst of all those pastel beaded gowns and stiff hairdos as a bold bird of paradise would among sweet and fragile magnolia blossoms.

As she and Michael got close enough to identify the women, Molly guessed they would ante up a good one thousand dollars apiece before Liza let them escape. Most would consider it a small price to pay to have their friends see them on the society page a few days from now.

Molly watched in amusement as Liza went into her hard sell.

"How does she do that?" Michael asked in wonder as checks changed hands.

"Liza has no shame when it comes to protecting the environment and any critter living in it. She will grovel, if she has to."

"How much do you figure an event like this will net?"

"Forty thousand, maybe more," she said as Michael's eyes widened. "If Liza had actually chaired the event, she would have tried to lure a couple of celebrities into town. With a little star power, she could have doubled the profits."

"Why didn't she go for it, then?"

"Because, as I understand it, the chairwoman did not take kindly to suggestions from her committee."

"The chairwoman is an egotistical idiot," Liza muttered under her breath as she joined them just in time to catch the gist of the conversation.

"She did manage to get all the upper-crust scions of the oldest Miami families to turn out," Molly reminded her.

"Sure, but she ignored the rest of the community," Liza countered. "If a few of us hadn't set out to corral people like you and Michael, we would have had to have a nurse on duty to hand out vitamins at the door or the whole crowd would have fallen asleep by nine."

"Don't you think you might be exaggerating

just a little bit?'' Molly asked. ''You're just miffed because you wanted Julio Iglesias to sing and she'd never heard of him.''

''Forget Julio Iglesias. I doubt I could have talked her into inviting Wayne Newton.'' She stood on tiptoe to kiss Michael's cheek. ''Thanks for coming, you two. Mingle. Have fun. I've got to go see if I can get old man Jeffries to cough up a few thousand bucks before he dies. I've heard he's willing to save the manatees. Maybe I can get him together with Jimmy Buffet and put together a benefit concert.''

Liza disappeared around a hedge, leaving the two of them staring after her.

''Where does she find the energy?'' Michael marveled.

''I think it takes about twenty minutes and the mention of a cause to recharge her batteries.'' Molly glanced up. ''Are you interested in checking out the buffet?''

He shook his head. A wicked gleam lit his dark brown eyes. ''Not right now. I'm more in the mood to shock this stuffy crowd.''

''Oh?'' Molly replied cautiously. The last time Michael had that look in his eyes he'd kissed her senseless.

''Follow me.''

He held out his hand, and after a momentary hesitation Molly took it. ''Exactly what do you have in mind?''

''I intend to start by removing selective pieces of clothing.''

She stopped in her tracks. ''You what?'' It wouldn't do to get too elated under the circumstances. She had a discouraging feeling he wasn't about to lure her into one of the mansion's many bedrooms and have his way with her.

He grinned. "Scared, Molly?"

"Of you? Never!" she declared staunchly.

"Then let's go."

As they crossed the lawn, Molly's pulse reached an anticipatory rate that would have her in the hospital down the block if it continued unchecked. The music drifted on the night breeze, swirling around them. The slow, romantic beat was counterpointed by laughter that grew more distant as they reached the shadowy fringes of the estate. Michael's hand curved reassuringly around hers.

"Put your hand on my shoulder," he instructed, standing before her. "Lift your foot."

"Is this anything like that game where you put different body parts on different squares until everyone ends up on the ground in a tangle?"

"Sounds fascinating," he said, "but no." He removed her shoe and tucked it in his pocket. "Other foot."

"Michael, I do not intend to romp around this place barefooted."

"Careful, sweetheart. Your stuffy social graces are showing."

In return for that remark, she nearly planted her spiked heel atop his foot. Unfortunately, as a volunteer soccer coach to say nothing of being witness to a fair amount of gunplay, Michael's reflexes tended to be lightning quick. He stepped nimbly aside. Molly's heel dug into the damp ground, which effectively removed her shoe just as he'd intended in the first place.

He glanced at her stocking-clad feet. "How about those?"

"Is this one of those kinky things I've read about?"

"Last I heard there wasn't anything kinky about sitting on a dock by the bay, but I'm game if you want to show me."

"You would be," she muttered darkly, trying not to let her disappointment show. Kinky with Michael O'Hara might have had its good points. She wasn't about to be the one to initiate it, though. She glanced at the coral rock ledge, then at the water lapping gently against it. "You don't actually expect me to sit on that, do you?"

"Of course not," he said, sweeping off his jacket and spreading it before her.

Molly had a hunch the gesture wasn't entirely due to gallantry. In fact, she was almost certain she heard him sigh with relief. She glanced from Michael to his quite probably ruined jacket, then to the water that seemed ominously dark in this shadowed corner.

"What do you suppose is in there?"

"A little seaweed. A few fish. Nothing to worry about."

"Maybe you don't consider having barracuda nibbling at your toes to be risky, but I'm not all that enchanted with the idea."

"I doubt there are any barracuda lurking down there."

"Not good enough," she said. "I want conviction in your voice or my toes stay on land."

"Ah, Molly. Where's the romance in your soul?" he murmured just close enough to her ear to give her goose bumps. His finger trailed along her neck, then over her bare shoulder.

Molly shivered. She was entirely too responsive and Michael was entirely too skilled at this seduction stuff. Another five minutes and the society grand dames truly would have something to shock the daylights out of them. As an alternative, Molly practically dove for the coral rock ledge. She stuck her feet, stockings and all, into the bathwater warm bay.

Michael's amused chuckle was entirely too predictable. As he sat down next to her she considered, for no more than an instant, tumbling him into the bay so he could cool off his . . . libido.

As if he guessed her thoughts, he grinned at her. "Don't even think about it," he said.

"What?" she inquired innocently. Suddenly something brushed past her foot, something considerably larger than a guppy or even a damned barracuda she thought, as a scream rose up in her throat and snagged.

"What," she asked in a choked voice, "what is that?"

"What is what?" Michael said, instantly alert to the change in her voice.

She was already standing, water pooling at her feet as she pointed at the murky depths. "There's something in there."

"Probably just some seaweed."

"I don't think so. It felt . . ." She was at a loss for an accurate description. "Slimy."

"That's how seaweed feels," he said, sounding so damned calm and rational she wanted to slug him.

"Does it also feel big?" she snapped.

"Big like a manatee? Maybe one is tangled in the mangroves."

Molly wasn't sure exactly how she knew that Michael was wrong, but she was certain of it. "Maybe we should go get a flashlight."

"By the time we do, I'm sure whatever it is will be gone."

"Michael, humor me. If it is a trapped manatee, we ought to free it or Liza will never forgive us. If it's . . . something else, we ought to do, hell, I don't know. Just get the flashlight. I'll wait here," she said before she realized that she'd be left alone with something that every instinct told her was very human and very dead.

Michael had taken two steps back toward the house, when she grabbed his arm. "Never mind. I'll go for the flashlight. Give me your car keys. You stay here."

His expression suddenly serious, he handed over the keys without argument, either to humor her or because his highly developed instincts for trouble had finally kicked in. "Don't say a word to anyone, Molly. There's no point in alarming everyone unnecessarily."

She nodded, then took off across the lawn, oblivious to the stares she drew as she raced barefoot through the guests, across the central courtyard of the house and down the driveway to the parking lot. It could have taken no more than ten minutes, fifteen at the outside, but it felt like an eternity before she made it back to where Michael was waiting. She'd grabbed a glass of champagne and chugged it down on the way. She had a hunch she was going to need it.

Michael took the flashlight from her trembling grasp and shone it onto the water in front of where they'd been sitting. At first it seemed she must have been mistaken as the glare picked up no more than a few strands of seaweed, a tangle of mangrove roots, a curved arm of driftwood. As the light skimmed across the surface and back again, Molly's heart suddenly began to thud.

"There," she whispered. "Move it back a little. See?"

What at first seemed to be no more than seaweed moved sensuously on the water's surface. It was a distinctive three-carat diamond that finally caught the light, broke it into a hundred shimmering rays, and removed any lingering doubts about the exact nature of Molly's discovery.

"Oh, my God," Molly whispered, her gaze fixed on the glittering ring that she herself had once coveted at a charity auction. Though her stomach was pitching acid, she forced herself to look again, just to be sure.

Michael's arm circled her waist. The flashlight wavered in his grasp and the light pooled at her feet, instead of on the water. "Are you okay?" he asked.

"As well as anyone would be after discovering

another body. For someone not even remotely interested in signing on for homicide investigations, I have a nasty suspicion I've seen almost as many murder victims as you have in the past few months.''

"Don't you think you're jumping to conclusions? We have no way of knowing whether the woman was murdered until we get the body out of there."

"Trust me," Molly said. "Tessa Lafferty would never willingly ruin her hairdo, to say nothing of her designer gown. If she felt ill, she would go home, send the dress to the secondhand store on consignment, and then climb between her two hundred dollar sheets and die. If she's in that water, it's because someone heaved her into the bay."

"Isn't Tessa Lafferty the woman Liza described as an idiot?"

She glared at him. "What are you suggesting?"

"Nothing. I'm just asking, purely for purposes of clarification, if it's the same woman."

"It is. But Liza would never kill her just because she didn't want some Latin singer that Liza has the hots for to sing at this bash."

"Did I say she would?"

"No, but I know how you think."

"Do you really? How is that?"

"Like a cop."

"Then I suppose you won't mind obeying an official request."

She regarded him warily. "Which is?"

"Go into the house and call the police."

"Only if you promise that Liza will not be on

the list of suspects you turn over to the Miami police."

"Sweetheart, you and I are on that list of suspects. Now move it."

Molly didn't waste time arguing that they provide tidy alibis for each other. She was more concerned with warning Liza that inviting a homicide detective to a charity function was just about the same as inviting trouble.

From the bestselling author of
The Naked Heart

JACQUELINE BRISKIN